Kathryn Foxfield scares people for a living. She's the bestselling author of the young-adult novels *Good Girls Die First*, *It's Behind You*, *Tag You're Dead* and *Getting Away with Murder*. *Things That Go Bump* is her first book aimed at terrifying younger readers.

When she's not daydreaming at her laptop, Kathryn likes to lurk in haunted caves, tacky tourist attractions and overgrown cemeteries. She lives in a sleepy Oxfordshire town with her partner, two children, a cat and a lizard.

BOOKS BY KATHRYN FOXFIELD
FOR OLDER READERS:

Good Girls Die First

It's Behind You

Tag, You're Dead

Getting Away With Murder

THINGS THAT GO BUMP

KATHRYN FOXFIELD

ILLUSTRATED BY
ROBIN BOYDEN

■ SCHOLASTIC

Published in the UK by Scholastic, 2024
1 London Bridge, London, SE1 9BG
Scholastic Ireland, 89E Lagan Road,
Dublin Industrial Estate, Glasnevin, Dublin, D11 HP5F

ISBN 978 0702 32499 4

A CIP catalogue record for this book
is available from the British Library.

Printed and bound in Great Britain by Clays Ltd, Elcograf S.p.A
Paper made from wood grown in sustainable forests
and other controlled sources.

MIX
Paper | Supporting
responsible forestry
FSC
www.fsc.org
FSC® C018072

1 3 5 7 9 10 8 6 4 2

www.scholastic.co.uk

For Eliza

FLASHLIGHT HIDE-AND-SEEK

"Come out, come out, wherever you are!"

I shine my torch into every cobwebbed corner. Shadows stretch up the walls like yawning monsters. It's the witching hour. That time just past midnight when the world is hazy and not quite real. The perfect time of night to play flashlight hide-and-seek.

My torch flickers off and I'm plunged into darkness. "Don't even think about it," I whisper, bashing it on my palm until the light flares bright again.

The floorboards creak beneath my feet as I sneak along the upstairs landing. Stacks of paper and piles of dirty washing are arranged in an obstacle course.

There's a stinky gym bag hanging from a door handle, casting a shadow that reminds me of a goblin.

A muffled giggle makes me stop. I think it came from the bathroom. Kicking open the door, I leap around the corner. "Got you!"

But there's no one in here. I shake the shower curtain in case Ada has somehow squirrelled herself away in the folds. I even lift the toilet lid and check inside.

"Where are you?" I mutter, starting to feel grumpy for not having found her yet. I check my watch. It's been seven minutes already – my record is three. I've carefully searched almost every room, ticking off all the potential hiding places in my head. It's a method that usually wins me this game. Tonight, though, something feels off.

Ada and I have been playing flashlight hide-and-seek since we were six years old. We've played it at every sleepover we've ever had. There have been a lot of sleepovers because our parents are best friends, which means Ada and I are best friends too. We didn't get any choice in the matter.

Sometimes I wonder if we would have become

friends on our own. Probably not. Ada and I are as different as they come. According to my teachers, I am *a pleasure to have in class*. Which means I'm so quiet they don't know what else to say about me. To the other kids at school, I'm *Ada's sidekick whose face goes red if you look at her.*

My name's Olive, by the way, but you'll probably forget.

I shine my torch into the mirror above the sink. The girl looking back at me has freckled white skin, messy brown hair and a worried expression. She looks kind of boring, if you ask me. Boring and forgettable.

No one could ever forget Ada. She's pale-skinned with red curly hair, extremely loud and has an opinion about everything. Also, she's usually dressed up like it's Halloween no matter what the occasion. I used to think she was the most interesting person in the world, but lately I've started noticing other people find her a bit weird and annoying. Which means they think *I'm* weird and annoying for being friends with her.

If I can't be invisible then I want to be normal. Ada makes both impossible.

I tiptoe past my dads' room – no one will be hiding in there – and approach the spiral staircase leading up to the loft. We had it converted into a spare bedroom a few months ago. Before then, the loft was a dark and creepy space full of scratchy yellow insulation and an entire spider civilization. I am still not over the spiders.

As I climb, I'm sure the temperature drops by a few degrees. At the top, I push open the door. "Ada?" I say.

There's no answer, but I can smell cola bottles. After eating three bags of pick 'n' mix, Ada is practically exhaling E-numbers, so I know she's somewhere in here.

"Got you now," I say, shining my torch around the room.

The beam of light snags on the sharp edges of a dozen cardboard boxes. Tall heavy boxes, short stumpy boxes, long flat boxes. An entire cityscape of cardboard boxes, all of them purchased on my family's most recent trip to the Flatpack superstore.

It's my dads' favourite shop. Flatpack sells everything, from self-assembly wardrobes and bookcases, to sofas and rugs, to kitchen and bathroom accessories, to lamps and toys. Dad and Papa get very overexcited when they go to Flatpack, and we always come home with at least ten things we didn't know we wanted.

Take last weekend. We went there to get new furniture for the loft conversion: a wardrobe, double bed, bookcase, drawers and a rug. In addition to the items we needed, we came home with: a cushion shaped like a llama, a set of nesting tables, six wine goblets and some plastic plants.

I squeeze past the gigantic box containing the new wardrobe. It's actually going back to the shop tomorrow because it smells funny. Like rotting leaves and wet earth. It basically smells like my dog after a trip to the woods. He always goes for an explore down by the stream and comes out coated in thick, stinky mud. That's the wardrobe smell: muddy dog.

Papa is annoyed the wardrobe has to go back. He wanted to get on with building it. Papa loves DIY. It's his number two hobby, right after watching 1980s films that give me nightmares. Dad also loves old films, but he hates DIY. He's happy the wardrobe has gone mouldy. A trip to Flatpack means he will get to buy the gold pineapple ornaments he was swooning over last week.

As I brush against the box, I feel something wet. I lift my hand and long strands of a sticky substance stretch between my fingers and the box. There's goo smeared around a ragged hole in the cardboard. I'm fairly sure it's snot. But whose snot? My number one suspect is Milo the dog.

"That's disgusting," I say, trying to wipe the snot on my leggings. It won't come off, though. I'm going to have to go and wash my hands. "Ada? Come out already. I've had enough of this game," I say.

She doesn't come out.

A scuttling sound makes me jump and I nearly drop the torch. Scuttling is an un-Ada-like noise. She's more of a stomper. "Are you in here?" I say nervously.

There's no answer.

All of a sudden, I feel cold and clammy. I can't shake the feeling I'm being watched. My teeth chatter and my tummy gurgles. It doesn't take much to scare me. Outwardly, I try to act like a normal eleven-year-old. One who isn't scared of practically everything. But on the inside, I'm in a constant state of terror.

"Ada, this isn't funny," I say.

The something scuttles again. I shine my torch between the boxes. It finds a hunched shape that unfolds itself under the light. I notice the monster's shadow first. There's a long, vicious spike on the top of its head.

It has a rounded snout and outstretched hands like it's reaching for me.

My thoughts run away with themselves, and I'm immediately imagining fangs dripping in blood. Claws for tearing meat. Tusks for goring its prey. What? I have a very active imagination and my parents' love for scary old films has only added fuel to the fire. I still have nightmares about *Jurassic Park* and *Jaws*.

"Grrr urggg," the thing says.

I scream and throw my torch. It clunks off the thing and somersaults to the floor, the light beam slashing across the ceiling.

"Ouch," the thing says. "What did you do that for?"

My brain finally catches up with my eyes, and I remember Ada is wearing her unicorn onesie. I get my fear back under control. The spike I saw silhouetted on the wall was her horn. There's no monster. I breathe out shakily.

"You made me jump," I say.

She cracks up laughing and switches on her torch. She uses it to light up her face from underneath. She's modified her onesie to give the once-cute unicorn vicious fangs, a pirate's eye patch and a bloodied horn. Ada likes to be unique.

"Your face was brilliant," she says. "I wish I'd caught it on camera."

"It's not nice to laugh at people," I say.

"I'm not laughing at you. I'm laughing at your *face*."

My fists clench at my sides. Part of me – a really big part of me – wants to yell at Ada. I want to tell her she's mean and it hurts when she mocks me for being scared. Shout at her that this isn't how friends treat each other.

But an even bigger part of me worries she'll laugh and tell me we're not *real* friends. It doesn't matter that we've known each other for nearly our whole lives. I can never shake the feeling that she doesn't genuinely like me, because why would someone like her want to be friends with someone like me?

My dads say I am the most wonderful, loveable, interesting person they've ever met. They tell me that anyone would be lucky to be my friend. Only they *have* to say those things. I suspect it's an actual requirement when you adopt a baby that you tell them how amazing they are on a daily basis.

That's why I don't yell at Ada. Instead, I force my fists to relax and unclench the knot in my stomach. "I think we should go back down—"

The horrible scuttling starts up again and interrupts me. It sounds like someone dragging their fingernails along cardboard.

"Did you hear something?" Ada says. She peers between the boxes.

"Are you doing that?" I ask. "It's not funny."

"Maybe it's a mouse," she says. "Or a super intense spider."

The sound comes again. This time, it's like claws slowly clicking on wooden floorboards. I'm pretty certain Ada is tapping her toe on the floor to make the noise. But I can't be a hundred per cent sure.

"I don't like this," I say. "Please, Ada."

Ignoring me, she drops to all fours. She crawls between the boxes, her rainbow tail trailing behind her. She points her torch into all the small gaps, not seeming to care what she might find. "Incy wincy spider," she sings, "climbed up the—"

Suddenly, a shadow grows up the wall. It looks like

a spider, only its legs have way too many joints and its body is covered in spikes. It's quivering, like it's getting ready to attack. Quite literally, it is the most terrifying thing I have ever seen.

"Ada, stop it!" I scream.

I don't know how she's making the shadow, but I need her to stop.

"Stop it, stop it, stop it."

The shadow twitches, then bolts. I scream and run for the stairs, only it's dark without my torch and my head clunks against the door frame. I land painfully on my bum. I can hear the *scuttling* again. Legs scratch against cardboard. There's a ripping, tearing noise. And ... squelching?

Then the noise stops and, somehow, this makes everything even more terrifying.

"Help," I scream. "Somebody help me."

All the lights come on and my parents burst in, wearing their matching Christmas PJs. Papa is brandishing a book as a weapon and Dad is waving his arms around like he's doing air karate.

"What's wrong?" Papa shouts. His glasses are on

upside down and his blonde hair is all tufty. "Who's hurt?"

Ada sticks her head up from behind a box. "There was a big spider," she says. "A monster spider."

Both my dads look at me, all crumpled up on the floor. "Olive?" Dad says, crouching down with a crack of his knees. "Are you OK?"

I nod and shake my hair forward to hide the bump on my head where I ran into the door frame. With the lights on, I can see how silly I was being. Of course there's no monster. But there *is* a big spindly plant sitting on top of a box, and I'm almost completely sure it was responsible for the shadow I saw.

"False alarm," I say quietly, not meeting Dad's tired brown eyes. He looks so worried and I feel so bad. "Sorry about waking you."

Papa huffs in mild irritation. "All right, bedtime. No more flashlight hide-and-seek."

He doesn't need to tell me. There's no way I am playing this game with Ada again, ever.

NO SUCH THING AS MONSTERS

I avoid Ada all weekend. She must think I'm ridiculous. I can't believe I panicked over a literal shadow and screamed the house down. I try to stop thinking about how embarrassed I am. This makes me think about it more.

I'm thinking about it on Saturday, when I go to Flatpack with my parents to return the stinky wardrobe. I'm thinking about it on Sunday morning, when I help Papa build its replacement. I'm thinking about it on Sunday afternoon, when I advise Dad on the placement of his new gold pineapple ornaments.

By Monday, I've thought about it so much I'm

convinced Ada's going to have the whole school laughing at me. My heart's doing somersaults as I walk into the classroom. Ada is already there. She's dressed for the occasion and is wearing non-regulation rainbow socks and about thirty hair clips in her red curls. She's sitting cross-legged on top of a table, talking to the new girl, Emily.

"It was a literal monster," Ada says.

"There's no such thing as monsters," Emily replies, sounding bored.

Emily started at our school a week ago and, so far, I've not gathered up the courage to speak to her even though we sit at the same table. She's incredibly intimidating. Like, she's the tallest person in the whole class and she has her blonde hair cut short like one of the boys. I would never dare do something that makes me stand out so much.

Emily doesn't care if she stands out. She speaks to everyone without going red in the face, even the teachers, and the whole school already knows who she is because she's epically good at sports. She plays hockey, football and tennis, and on her first day here, she beat everyone in the daily mile even though it's not supposed to be a race.

She's the coolest person I've ever met, which makes her terrifying.

The thought of Emily laughing at me because of the monster thing makes my breakfast bubble in my tummy. So I get out my reading book and slide silently into my chair, hoping Ada and Emily are too busy talking to notice me. They notice me.

Ada swats the book out of my hands. "Olive saw the monster too, didn't you, Olive?"

Emily raises an eyebrow at me.

"I think it was a plant's shadow," I reply quietly, grabbing my book back. I'm reading *The Princess Bride*, which was turned into one of Dad's favourite films. The book's not as scary as the film, mostly because it doesn't contain any shrieking eels. Sometimes it feels like I'm the only person in the world who doesn't love monsters.

"What?" Ada cries. "No! You definitely saw it, I know you did. You screamed like you thought you were going to die."

Her voice is so loud that everyone else in the class

stops their own conversations and stares at us. My face turns red-hot, waiting for the laughter that doesn't come. I think everyone is too shocked to laugh.

"Admit you saw the monster," Ada shouts. "Admit it!"

One of the popular boys – Jack – abandons his friends and slouches into the seat next to me. A glitter tattoo sparkles on his dark brown arm. It's a spider, of all things. I shiver and look away.

"Monsters, huh?" he says, grinning. "Tell me more, ladies."

"Urgh, don't call us ladies," Emily says. "It's so patronizing."

"Forgive me, my queen," Jack says. He puts on a posh accent and bows to Emily. "I meant no disrespect."

"Slightly better," Emily says, sniffing. She shuffles around in her chair and looks him up and down. "What's your name again?"

Jack acts like she's stabbed him in the heart and falls to the floor. Emily glances over at me and winks. She knows his name. Everyone knows his name. The only person in our class who is louder than Ada is Jack. It's impossible to ignore him.

"Jack's dead," Finn shouts from across the room. "He's been murdered."

A few people cheer. Krish tries to start a conga line, but no one else joins in.

"Can I have his Switch?" Oscar says.

"No, it's going to be buried with me," Jack says, climbing back on to his chair.

He pats his hair, like he's checking the twists haven't been knocked out of position. Jack likes to look perfect at all times. One day, he's going to be a famous YouTuber. For now, he's in training mode, as he puts it. This involves him talking with a bad American accent and waving his arms around a lot, like he's bringing a plane in for landing.

"The one and only Jack York at your service," he says, introducing himself to Emily. "I saw you playing football in the park yesterday. You're good."

Emily shrugs. "Yeah, I know. Do you play?"

Jack laughs like this is the funniest joke in the world. "Do I ... do I play football?" His laughter stops abruptly. "No. I most certainly do not."

17

Jack's about as sporty as I am and spends most PE lessons messing around. Everyone still wants to be on his team. This has never made sense to me, despite all my efforts to understand the mysteries of popularity. I've rated all my classmates based on how many friends they have. I've analysed the things they talk about. I've made endless lists, because a good list usually solves any problem. Nothing adds up.

Ada raps her knuckles on the table and makes me jump. "Can we get back to our conversation?"

"What conversation?" Emily says.

"The monsters!" Jack exclaims. "Which, in case you weren't aware, is *totally* my bag. I'm a massive gamer and horror is everything to me. Everything."

"Do you always speak like that?" Emily asks.

"Like what?"

"Like you're being filmed."

"Yes," Jack and I say in unison.

The three of them turn to look at me, apparently surprised I spoke. I clear my throat and bury myself in my book.

Ada sighs loudly. "If everyone could stop interrupting

me for one second," she says. "I was explaining how Olive and I saw a real monster on Friday."

"It was the shadow of a plant," I say, but no one hears me.

"I've been doing some research and the monster definitely came from Flatpack." Ada cranes her head to check Mrs Butcher is still outside, talking to a parent. Then she breaks one of the school's biggest rules and takes out her phone. "Check out these reviews I found."

Jack takes the phone and holds it so we can all see. He scrolls through a page of reviews of Flatpack products. Ada has narrowed them down to ones that include the word "haunted" in the text. To my surprise, there are dozens of them.

Jack reads one out. "We bought a wardrobe but were disappointed to undo the packaging and discover that not only did it smell like death, but it also appeared to be haunted." He laughs loudly, slapping his hand on the table. "Haunted. Amazing."

Ada takes the phone back. "Hashtag Haunted Flatpack was briefly trending on social media a few weeks ago," she says. "People were saying that

after buying Flatpack furniture, weird stuff started happening in their homes. Like, scary shadows and scuttling sounds at night."

"Ohhh, creepy," Emily says sarcastically.

"I'm serious," Ada continues. "Loads of people have had to return wardrobes to the shop because they believed they were haunted. Olive's dads took theirs back on Saturday. Right, Olive?"

"Because it smelt of fungus," I mumble. "It was mouldy, not haunted."

"Answer me this, did the store seem surprised when you returned it?" Ada says, flicking a rogue curl out of her eyes. "Or did they act like they were used to people bringing back their *haunted* wardrobes?"

Now that she mentions it, the staff didn't ask any questions. They processed our refund and one of them made a quick walkie-talkie call. What was it he said? *We've got another one for Warehouse Two.* Something like that.

"Well?" Ada says.

"Um, well, they gave us our money back and a new wardrobe for free, so—"

"Exactly!" she shouts. "It's a conspiracy! They're covering something up, and that something is an infestation of literal monsters. Don't try to deny it, Olive."

"I, um—"

"See, she agrees," Ada says smugly. "Case closed."

"Let her speak for herself," Emily says. "You're always talking over her."

She looks at me with one raised eyebrow, waiting patiently for me to either confirm or deny Ada's theory. I'm not used to people wanting to hear what I have to say. It's horrifying being put on the spot, but also … kind of nice?

Normally, I'd go along with whatever Ada says. Only, I don't think I want to this time. Emily doesn't know me yet. She doesn't know anyone. This could be my chance to be who I want to be for once. Instead of Ada's sidekick, I can be Olive. Someone with opinions of her own.

My imagination runs away with itself. I picture Emily deciding she wants to be my friend, all based on what I say next. It genuinely feels like a moment in time that could change my entire life. Like in the old film *Back to the Future*, when one of the characters stands up to a bully and it rewrites their whole story.

Ada's not a bully – she's just a bit bossy. But I still feel like me picking what *I* want for once has the power to change *everything*. This is my *Back to the Future*, rewrite-my-whole-story moment. I could go from feeling like the strange, shy girl who no one really knows, to someone with real friends. Friends like Emily, not Ada. Friends who actually like me.

So I draw myself up in my chair and take a deep breath. "Grow up, Ada," I say, my voice shaky. "Only little kids believe in haunted wardrobes. There's no such thing as monsters."

A few people laugh nervously and that's when I realize the whole class was listening in. Ada's face goes bright red to match her hair. She stares at me with her mouth hanging open. She's either angry or upset, I can't tell the difference. Then she slides off the table and pushes her way through the classroom, to the toilets.

"Burn," Jack says, wincing.

"Why is everyone out of their seats?" Mrs Butcher

says, walking into the classroom.

Jack scurries off to rejoin his table. All of his friends look at me as they whisper behind their hands. Oh no. I think I might have confused standing up for myself with being mean. I stare at the door through which Ada vanished and try to gather up the courage to go after her. Mrs Butcher is about to start the register, though.

"She's being dramatic," Emily says. "She'll get over it."

Ada doesn't get over it. She asks Mrs Butcher if she can move tables and she sits next to a boy called Rube. It turns out I was right, and what I said did change my life. Because in that moment, Ada stopped wanting to be my friend.

A TERRIBLE IDEA

Being friends with Emily hasn't fixed my whole life.

It's been two whole months since my break-up with Ada, and nothing has changed. I've just swapped one friend who doesn't really like me for another. Ada's been replaced with Emily, but I still feel like a sidekick. A sidekick to someone who I don't have anything in common with.

Emily's not watched any of the old films I love. I've not watched any of the sporting events she loves. She doesn't know who E.T. is, and I don't know who Lauren James is. When we hang out, we talk about people at school and that's it. We don't hang out much, though. She's always busy doing sporty stuff I can't join in with.

At playtime, I usually end up sitting alone, watching Emily play football. I'd thought being her friend would mean some of what makes her amazing would rub off on me. But in the last two months, I've not magically become a more popular, more interesting person. No, I've stayed exactly the same, with the added bonus that Ada now hates me.

My eyes find Ada across the playground. She's sitting against the reading shed with her new friend Rube. They're hunched over a notebook. Ada is talking and Rube is nodding along. They're definitely up to something. I never thought I would miss being part of Ada's schemes, but I do.

"They're definitely up to something," Jack says, slumping next to me on the grass. He keeps doing this: talking to me, even when Emily's not around. They're best friends now, in case you're wondering. Emily's only been at my school for a couple of months, and she already has more friends than I've ever had.

"What do you think they're plotting?" Jack asks.

I chew my lip. Ada is always plotting something. The only difference is she's now doing it with my replacement, Rube. I take stock of him from a distance. He's small, with light brown skin and dark hair that he gels into a severe side-parting. He smiles a lot and he talks a lot.

I can't help but think he's probably a better sidekick than I was. I think he's definitely more interesting. He's into nature and knows about a million animal facts. I doubt he's as good at making plans as I am. But he probably makes up for it by not being scared of absolutely everything.

"Let's spy on them," Jack says, dragging me to my feet. "Em! Emily!"

Emily's busy winning her football match. She shoots for goal and scores. It's only when she's finished celebrating that she jogs over to us, pink-cheeked and muddy-legged. "What's up?"

"We need you," Jack says. "We're going on a dangerous mission to discover what Ada and Rube are up to."

For a moment, it looks like she's going to return to the football match. So it makes my heart flutter when she picks us instead. "I'm in," she says, wiping her grubby hands on her school shirt. "Let's sneak around behind them."

Ada can't hear us from where she's sitting, but she must sense our stares because she looks up. She glares at me, then moves so she's facing away from us.

We try to act casual as we cross the playground. Emily loops one arm through mine and her other through Jack's. We pretend we're going on the exercise equipment. I can see Ada and Rube out of the corner of my eye, but I can't hear them.

"I've got an idea," Jack says. "As soon as Mrs Scout is looking the other way, run for the shed. Now! Go, go, go."

He scampers towards the reading shed and disappears behind it. I didn't sign up for this. Everyone knows we're not allowed behind the reading shed, it's one of the school rules. Last year, Rube hid down there after getting upset watching a nature documentary about endangered armadillos. It was thirty minutes before he was found, by which point our teacher had already called the police. The next day, we had an assembly entirely about not hiding when we're sad, and it was made very clear that behind the shed is a no-go area. We're going to get into loads of trouble if we're caught.

"I don't think we should—" I start to say.

"Don't worry," Emily says. "No one will see us."

I have no choice but to slip into the narrow space. It's full of cobwebs, which makes me even more nervous. Spiders. Yuck. We step over punctured footballs and plastic flowerpots left here by Gardening Club. I trip over a skipping rope and my face bumps into Jack's back.

"That was an accident!" I say. "I didn't touch you on purpose."

Jack acts like nothing happened. "I can't hear what they're saying. I'm going to try to get closer." He squeezes out from behind the shed. "Commando roll!" he cries. Then he somersaults into the wall, remaining upside down with his legs in the air. So much for being sneaky.

"Err, what?" Ada says, putting down her notebook.

"You can't see me," Jack says, scrambling on to his hands and knees. He crawls away as fast as he can. "I am a figment of your imagination."

Emily pushes me from behind and I awkwardly shuffle out of our hiding place. I avoid meeting Ada's eye, but I know she's glowering at me.

"What do you three want?" she snaps.

"You're sus," Emily says, sitting down opposite Ada and Rube. "We're being good citizens by finding out what you're up to."

Jack sits too, and picks bits of dry grass off his neatly ironed polo shirt. "That was surprisingly painful. So, what's happening?"

Ada doesn't answer. Instead she looks up at me with narrowed eyes. I lurk nervously next to the shed with my arms folded. I don't want to get any closer. Over the past two months, Ada and I have become matching magnetic poles. We have so much shared history, but it acts to push us apart rather than bring us together.

Rube clears his throat. "We're going to discover a new species. You probably think science knows about all of the animals on Earth, but hundreds of new creatures are discovered every year. It's fascinating."

"Just a guess, but I don't think you're going to find

any undiscovered species in this playground," Jack says. "Unless you count Mrs Scout."

"Do you remember that spider monster you didn't see?" Ada says, talking to me. "The one that didn't exist because there's no such thing as monsters?"

I shake my head and stare at my feet.

"We've been doing some research, and my theory was correct. There really are monsters living at Flatpack, and we're going to get proof."

"My aunt's a cleaner at Flatpack," Rube says. "There's a big staff party in a few weeks. It's being held at the Five Seasons Hotel, so the store is closing early."

"We're going to get ourselves locked in overnight," Ada says.

Jack and Emily exchange slow grins. Emily leans over to whisper something in Jack's ear, and his grin widens. "Tell us more about this plan," he says.

Ada shrugs. "That is the plan."

"That's not a plan," I say.

Everyone looks at me. I wouldn't normally speak up, but plans are my thing. If I had to describe myself in three words, it would be panic, plans and old films. All right, that's more than three words, but you know what I mean.

I take a deep breath. "That's an *idea*. But you haven't considered any of the specifics. Like what about security cameras and alarms? How exactly are you going to get locked in without anyone noticing you? What about your schedule? Do you have an equipment list? A first-aid kit? A map of the store?"

Ada rolls her eyes like I'm ruining her fun by being too sensible.

I lift my chin at her. For once I am the one who knows what they're talking about. "Without a proper plan, you'll be thrown out within minutes and banned from the store."

Rube nods. "I think Olive has a point. Maybe we should think it through a bit better."

"There's no time. The staff party is once a year, so this is our only chance." She snatches up her notebook and stuffs it into the waistband of her shorts.

Emily leans over to whisper in Jack's ear again. "Yes! That would be amazing," he says.

"What would be amazing?" Ada snaps.

"We're going to help you," Emily says.

"No, you're not," Ada says.

"Come on," Jack says. "One of my biggest dreams is to spend the night in that store, sleeping in the beds, pooing in the toilets."

Rube raises his hand. "The toilets aren't plumbed in."

"I don't care," Jack says. "Let me have my dream."

"You need us," Emily says. "You need Olive. She's the queen of plans. You won't pull it off without her and you know it."

"Wait, what?" I gasp. They want me to help them break the law by trespassing on Flatpack property? Me? I don't break rules. Even the *thought* of breaking a rule brings me out in a rash.

I'm reminded of one time when I accidentally dropped my apple in the park and it rolled past the STAY OFF THE GRASS sign. I ended up standing there for half an hour, torn over which rule to break: walking on the grass or littering.

"We'll win her over, don't worry," Emily says.

"You focus on the monster hunting and we'll arrange everything else."

Ada screws up her mouth like she's sucking on a lemon. I can see she's trying to pick between wanting to tell us all to go away and knowing I'm her only hope. She briefly glances at me and pulls a disgusted face. "I'll believe it when I see it," she sniffs, which is her way of agreeing to Emily's proposal.

Jack and Emily wait until Ada and Rube are gone, then they gesture for me to sit with them on the grass. "OK, this is going to be off the scale," Jack says. "I have so many ideas, my head is going to pop."

"I don't understand," I say. "Do you believe the monsters are real?"

"Of course not!" Emily laughs.

"But Ada and Rube think they are," Jack says.

"I still don't get it," I say.

"We're going to prank them!" Jack explains. "We're going to make them think the monsters do exist and get some sweet footage of them being all terrified for my channel. It will be hilarious."

"Will it?"

It doesn't sound hilarious to me. It sounds kind of mean. Then again, a lot of Jack's pranks feel mean to me. He does stuff like loosening the lid of someone's water bottle so they get soaked when they try to drink. Or one time he replaced the cream in a biscuit with toothpaste and gave it to someone to eat. But his victims always seem to laugh along. Maybe I don't have a very good sense of humour.

"You have to help us," Emily says. "You're good at plans. You think of everything."

"Please," Jack says, fluttering his eyelashes at me. "Please, please, please."

"Please, Olive, please," Emily says. "We'll love you forever."

I feel myself going red at all the attention. I've never been very good at saying no when I'm put on the spot. I should say no. I should definitely say no. But then I start thinking how this could be my chance to show everyone I'm not the boring one. I *can* be fun and adventurous.

Besides, if I don't do it, Emily might go and have this big Flatpack adventure with Ada and then she'll become Ada's friend, not mine. I can't lose both of them.

"OK," I say, already regretting my choice. "I'll help."

A LIST FOR EVERYTHING

Two weeks fly by and, before I know it, it's the day of the Flatpack staff party. We arrive an hour before closing time. The superstore car park is rammed as the doors belch out a steady stream of families overladen with screaming toddlers, value-for-money furniture and 75p meatpops.

A meatpop is like a lollypop, only it's made of – you guessed it – meat. Beef and chicken, to be precise, along with various other ingredients that don't sound like stuff you should be eating. Almost everyone buys a meatpop on the way home, and almost everyone regrets it. It's the texture. And the flavour. And the fact it looks like dried-out poo on a stick.

"Standing is making me hungry," Jack says, eyeing a bin full of half-eaten meatpops.

"Seriously?" I gape at him. "You've eaten one before, right?"

"Nope. My parents won't let me. But the smell of hot fat and spices calls to my soul." He inhales deeply and makes a long "ahhhhh" sound.

A woman leans past me to throw her meatpop in the bin. Jack moves towards it.

"No," Emily says. "Eating out of a bin is not *inconspicuous*. Rule One of Operation Flatpack, right, Olive?" She holds up a hand to high-five me.

It's Rule Two, but I let it go. At least she's sort of paid attention to the list of rules I sent her.

The *actual* Rule One of Operation Flatpack is we don't talk about Operation Flatpack. Basically, no mention of monsters where someone could hear us. My whole plan relies on us acting like innocent, harmless eleven-year-olds who are popping into the canteen for a snack. The Flatpack canteen is always full of kids, so it will be easy for us to blend into the crowd.

Which brings me to Rule Two. Be inconspicuous.

Jack is already breaking this rule thanks to his outfit. Emily's in her usual sportswear and I'm in leggings and a T-shirt. Jack, however, has decided to wear a bright yellow velvet blazer and pink trousers, which is a definite *choice*. He's so colourful that a million wasps are currently circling him, thinking he's a flower. I hate wasps. The bin next to us is full of them, crawling over the discarded meatpops.

"Since when do wasps eat meat?" I say, mostly to myself. "That one is literally chewing on a meatpop."

"Little known but fascinating fact," a voice says. "Wasps have teeth they use to eat other insects. And meat meant for human consumption, if they can find it."

We all look round and notice Rube is standing behind us. I don't know how long he's been there.

"That's horrifying," Emily says.

I don't know if she means Rube's outfit or his fact about wasps. Like Jack, Rube has broken Rule Two. He's dressed from head to toe in camouflage. It looks like he's planning to go on a jungle expedition. He's even got a backpack almost as big as he is.

"*Vespula vulgaris* is a very misunderstood species," Rube says. "In the UK alone, wasps capture over ten thousand tons of insects, including many garden pests. That's the equivalent of a hundred blue whales."

"Er, what?" Jack says.

"Without wasps, the world would be overrun with spiders." He shifts his bag on his shoulders, wincing under its weight. "As it is, an average house contains between fifty and three hundred spiders. Imagine if—"

"Can we not talk about spiders?" I say quickly.

Rube's face goes a bit red. "Yes. Of course. Sorry."

"Why's your bag so big?" Jack says.

"It's all our monster-hunting equipment. I've got motion-activated cameras, torches, audio-recording devices and temperature sensors. Also, cheese sandwiches and vegetable sticks."

"Good choice, good choice," Jack says, nodding. "I've got hot and spicy tortilla chips and four bottles of blue Quench. It's important to stay hydrated."

"Rule One," I hiss, gesturing for them to stop talking.

"Don't talk about Operation Flatpack," Rube says, looking smug.

"What's Rule Three again?" Jack asks.

"Um…?" Emily snaps her fingers. "Follow the rules!"

Something makes me think they are mocking my rules, but I can't be sure.

I take out my handwritten plan and read through the twenty-six phases. Phase One was meeting here, by this exact bin, at exactly 6 p.m. Phase Two was ordering snacks in the canteen. Phase Two was supposed to begin at 6.05 p.m. Except Ada is late and it is pushing everything off schedule.

I check my watch. It is now 6.11 p.m. If she doesn't turn up soon, the whole operation will be ruined. "I think we should go inside and wait in the canteen," I say. "We're drawing too much attention to ourselves out here."

"Let's go find some monsters!" Jack cries, making me cringe.

Several last-minute shoppers rushing inside the store turn to look at us. Oh no, Jack's already given us away!

"Monster *meatpops*," Emily says loudly. "We love meatpops!"

"Everyone stop speaking," I hiss.

We hurry through the big pink archway with our heads down. Flatpack's entrance hall is noisy, colourful and disorientating. The focal point is the huge escalator in the middle, carrying people upstairs to the showroom. There are signs everywhere that announce all the special offers and bargains. Furniture has been mounted on the walls and ceiling. Several shelving units are suspended at funny angles from big wires.

Flatpack's very similar to that other, infinitely nicer furniture megastore. It doesn't do anything quite as well though, meaning there are already queues and bottlenecks of people before you even reach the showroom. The noise and the colour scheme and the crowds make me feel like my head's stuck in a scratchy wool jumper. I want to tear it off and hurl it far away from me. I want everything to stop for a moment so I can think.

"Are you OK?" Rube says, blinking at me with his brown eyes magnified behind his glasses. He looks genuinely worried, which is embarrassing. I hadn't realized my discomfort was so obvious.

I pull myself together and force a smile. "Yeah, I'm good," I say. "Let's go upstairs."

We let the tide of people carry us up the escalator. To our left is the entrance to the showroom floor. To the right, the canteen. We find a table by the window. It's nice up here. Airy and bright thanks to the wall of glass overlooking the car park. Sure, it's a riot of chinking cutlery and crying toddlers. But for eleven-year-olds who eat their lunch in a school canteen five days a week, it's almost peaceful.

"Rock, paper, scissors to decide who goes to order," Emily says.

I glance at the giant queue and shudder. We pair up to play the first round. Best of three, winner advances to the final. It's me versus Jack, and Emily versus Rube.

"Rock, paper, scissors, shoot," the four of us say in unison, bashing our fists on our palms.

"Unicorn?" Jack says.

Unicorn isn't an approved shape. We've been through this many times with Jack. He's always trying to add in new moves, such as T. rex and zombie. Unicorn is new.

"You can't have unicorn," I say wearily.

"No, out there," he says, physically moving my head to make me look outside. "There's a unicorn in the car park."

I hate to say it, but he's right. And the unicorn in question is none other than my ex-best friend, Ada.

WHAT ARE YOU KIDS UP TO?

The whole canteen stops eating and watches Ada when she walks in. She's in her unicorn onesie: the one covered in fake blood. On top of that, her bright orange hair is escaping from under the hood like some kind of tentacled monster. To say she stands out is an understatement. When she spots me across the room, she tosses a cola bottle sweet into the air, her mouth opening wide to catch it.

"Does she not understand the word inconspicuous?" I mutter.

Rube taps me on the shoulder. "She's making a point. About how she doesn't have to do what you tell her.

Because you're not friends any more?"

"Yes, we got that part," Emily says, sighing.

None of the others know this, but Ada's not only

making a point about how I can't order her around. She's wearing the same outfit she had on *that* night. The night when she believes we saw a monster in my spare room. But I've run through what happened over and over. It can't possibly have been real. There was no spider shadow. Just a pair of eleven-year-olds who'd eaten too much sugar and stayed awake for too long.

The smell of Ada's cola bottles hits me as she reaches us. It's another reminder of *that* night. "Ready to find some monsters?" she says, loudly enough that the people at the next table look over.

"Rule One!" I say.

"You're breaking Rule One by bringing up Rule One," Ada says.

I don't have a comeback for this because, strictly speaking, it's true.

She checks her watch. "No time for snacks, let's get this show on the road," she says.

"What about the meatpops?" Jack says sadly.

"What about the plan?" I say. Everything is falling apart and we've not even begun yet.

Ada pulls Rube's arm. "Let's go."

Rube looks torn, but he quickly picks Ada. Only, when he tries to get up from his chair, he knocks over his massive bag and everything spills out across the floor. An infrared thermometer, a remote-control car on which Rube has duct-taped a camera, a Ouija board, and a bag of cheese sandwiches all go in different directions.

"Sorry! I'm so sorry." Rube crawls under the neighbouring table, gathering up the gear. It sounds like he's hiccuping. I start to worry he's going to cry. I start to worry *I'm* going to cry.

"What on Earth?" A woman at the table stands up and accidentally kicks Rube's infrared thermometer. It skitters away.

"Mommy!" Rube cries, hitting his head on the underside of the table. "I mean, my thermometer. Mommy is what I call him. It!"

"You named your thermometer?" Emily says.

"I'll get it," I say. "Just stop talking. All of you."

I crawl on my hands and knees towards the thermometer. It's lying by the window. I reach for it, but a clean white plimsoll gets in the way. A man towers over me. He's wearing the Flatpack uniform of khaki shorts, a pink polo shirt and neon orange jacket. He reminds me of an action figure, with his small waist and oversized biceps. He picks up the thermometer.

"What is this?" he asks, examining it from every angle. His voice is much higher than I expected, like he's an eleven-year-old boy trapped in a thirty-year-old man's body.

I don't know what to say, so I crawl backwards and rejoin the rest of the group. I glance over my shoulder, looking for a way out of this mess. My heart nearly jumps out of my mouth. The same man is now standing right behind us! It takes a second to realize there are two of them. They look *exactly* the same, down to their Ken doll blonde hair.

"Is Flatpack cloning its workers now?" Jack says. "Awesome."

"They're twins," I whisper. Now I've had a chance to look more closely, I can see the badges on their uniforms read MY NAME IS BILL and MY NAME IS BOB. The badges are the only difference between the two men.

"Identical twins are only commonly seen in humans and the nine-banded armadillo," Rube says. "It's incredibly rare in the animal kingdom as a whole. Actually, in dogs—"

"Now's not the time," Ada says, interrupting him. She stands on tiptoes and looks around the canteen. Something tells me she's about to do something that isn't in my plan.

"What are you kids up to?" the twin called Bill asks.

"Um, we have a perfectly reasonable explanation," Rube squeaks.

"One that definitely doesn't involve looking for monsters," Jack says. "Flatpack is definitely *not* haunted."

"Seriously?" Emily says.

"I'm not good at lying under pressure," Jack hisses.

I'm not good at *thinking* under pressure. My brain is shouting "Run, run, run" at me. Only I can't run because the two Flatpack workers are blocking both paths out of the canteen.

A loud whistle cuts through my panic. I look around and see Ada has jumped up on to a table. "You're all living a lie, sheeple," she shouts. "You're buying stuff you don't need, to fill the holes in your empty lives."

"Oh my gosh, is this her version of helping?" Emily says. "What is wrong with that girl?"

But in Ada's defence, it does take everyone's attention off the rest of us. "Consumerism is destroying the planet by convincing us we need all these *things* to make us happy. But it doesn't make us happy. It ends up in landfill and polluting the ocean."

"Get down from there," one of the twins shouts, marching towards her.

She grabs a white pineapple salt shaker and holds it aloft. "This isn't a tasteful table decoration. It is a sea turtle murder weapon!"

"Er, it's flimsy plastic. I don't think you could kill a turtle with that," Jack says. "Maybe a small fish if you threw it really hard."

"It breaks apart in the ocean," Rube says, his voice cracking. "When the turtles ingest the plastic, it clogs up their digestive systems and they die." His bottom lip wobbles.

"That's sad. All right, let's go," Emily says.

With the twins distracted by Ada, we have the chance to slip out of the canteen unnoticed. But Rube hesitates. "What about Mom ... my thermometer?" he whispers.

"Ada will buy you a new one," Emily says, steering him through the tables.

We nearly make it, but one of the twins notices us as we reach the canteen exit. "Hey, wait," he squeaks.

"Run," Jack says, taking off without us.

The original plan was to sit in the canteen until right before closing time. Then we'd sneak into the showroom and find somewhere to hide. There we'd wait for all the staff to leave, before finally emerging.

My plan has been ruined.

We run after Jack and I desperately try to come up with a new plan. Only Jack is holding his phone at arm's length, screaming dramatically into the camera. It makes it incredibly hard for me to think.

Ada catches us up at the entrance on to the showroom floor and we all skid into the first zone. We find ourselves surrounded by indoor plants. It looks like a jungle, with greenery hanging from the rafters and walls, and lined up on shelves.

There are all these posters talking about the benefits of bringing nature into your home. *Breathe easier! Reduce stress levels! Increase productivity! Be more creative!* I spot an immediate issue. All of the plants are plastic.

There's no time to think about this, though – we need to find somewhere to hide. Which is impossible when there are so many people walking incredibly slowly through the zone. Don't they realize the store is closing soon and they've still got a kilometre of showroom to walk through?

"No time to wait," Emily says, pulling both me and Jack towards a table covered in trailing plants. The leaves cascade to the floor like a waterfall of green. "Under here."

Emily, Jack and I dive under the table, but there's no room for Rube and Ada.

"Don't worry about us," Ada snaps. "We'll find our own spot."

"Happy hiding," Jack says, waving through the dangling foliage. "Don't let the monsters bi—"

"*Shush*," Emily says, clamping her hand over Jack's mouth.

Two pairs of identical calves appear on the other side of the leaf curtain. They're tanned and covered in blonde hairs. Their owners are both wearing neon

pink Flatpack-issued socks pulled up as high as they will go and perfectly white shoes. It's the twins, Bob and Bill.

"Where did they go, bro?" one of the twins asks in his little boy voice.

"Let's try living rooms, bro," an identical voice replies.

They both run off, their footsteps falling in unison. I don't hear any shouting, so hopefully they've not found Ada and Rube. Once I'm sure they're gone, I breathe out heavily. I nod at Emily and she removes her hand from Jack's mouth.

"That was brilliant," he immediately says. "I reckon I got some great footage."

"You spent the whole time screaming at your camera," I say.

"Yeah, exactly. I'm going to edit it with some scary music and clips of those terrifying Flatpack clones. Do you want to check it out?"

I ignore Jack and Emily as they watch Jack's footage on his phone. I take my list from my pocket and read through the original plan. We've broken all of my rules.

The schedule is completely ruined. We're being chased by Flatpack workers.

The sensible decision would be to cut our losses and go home. But I already know no one else will agree with me. Screwing up the plan, I stuff it back into my pocket. Fine. If the others are going to ignore all my hard work, then they can work things out for themselves. We'll see how far they get.

"We're not very well hidden," Emily says, nudging me. "Do you think we should hide somewhere else?"

I don't answer. I'm too irritated.

"We're totally going to get spotted," Jack says. "I'm too vibrant."

"That's one way of putting it," Emily says, laughing. "We'll give it a few minutes, then sneak into living rooms. It's the next zone."

"Yes! There will be cupboards or sofas we can hide behind." He high-fives her.

I sniff. This would have been my suggestion. Maybe they don't need me, after all. Coming here is the naughtiest thing I've done in my entire life and it was for nothing.

Jack rubs his hands together. "Bring on Phase Two of Operation Flatpack."

"We've done Phase Two," I grumble. "That was entering the store."

"I mean, Phase *Fun*," Jack clarifies. He pulls a plastic spider and a torch from his pocket. "Let's get scary."

A KAREN IN THE WILD

We scramble out through the trailing leaves and fall into step with a large group of shoppers. A couple of them glance at us but they don't say anything. Everyone's used to children treating Flatpack like a giant playground.

Proving my point, there are a couple of small kids running around with plastic plants on their heads, pretending to be sea monsters. Another two are trying to climb a trellis. I think they want to get up on to the criss-cross wooden beams that support all the partition walls. Their parents are too busy arguing over vases to notice.

It's basically chaos out here and I find myself missing

the space under the table. Everyone is desperately filling their trolleys and selecting warehouse items using the Flatpack app. They're all trying to finish their shopping before the store closes. As if twenty minutes is enough time. The showroom can literally steal hours from your day.

There's a big pink line painted on the floor that you're meant to follow – everyone calls it the Pink Brick Road. The Pink Brick Road deliberately takes you on the longest route possible, forcing you to weave through all the zones. My theory is this wears you down to the point where you're prepared to buy almost anything just to escape.

That's how it makes me feel anyway.

There are shortcuts everywhere, but they're not signposted. Flatpack wants people to get lost in here. It wants them to stay for as long as possible because then they'll buy more things. If you're going to waste four hours of your life, you need something to show for it at the end.

A voice speaks over the public address system. "This store will be closing in fifteen minutes. Please make your way to the collection area to pick up your warehouse items."

I feel a jolt of panic. It won't be long until the showroom empties out. We need to find a place to hide before it's too late. I risk stepping off the Pink Brick Road to overtake a slow-moving group of shoppers. Only, I must take a wrong turn because I find myself standing in front of a corridor closed off with a retractable belt barrier. A door reads: THE FLATPACK STORY.

"It's a new museum," Emily says. "My mum was telling me about it."

"A Flatpack museum?" Jack gasps. "Could this place be any more exciting?"

I'm not sure if he's being sarcastic or he's genuinely hyped to learn about the store's history. I don't get to ask. Right at that moment, the door opens and a store worker comes out. She's a white woman in her forties with short brown hair highlighted with sharp blonde streaks.

She jumps when she sees us. Then she composes herself and looks between the three of us. She lifts a walkie-talkie to her mouth. "Bob? Bill? What did you say those kids looked like?"

A crackly high-pitched voice replies. "There's five of them. A girl in sportswear, a boy wearing a velvet jacket, a unicorn and a small boy with a massive bag."

"That's four," the woman says.

"We can't remember what the last one looked like."

They're talking about me. Like I said, I'm very unmemorable.

The woman glances between Jack and Emily, and obviously decides we match the description well enough. "Where are your friends?" she barks. "You are all in so much trouble."

"I've never met a real one," Jack says.

He's staring at her with a look of awe. That's when I realize her name badge says MY NAME IS KAREN. Jack is obsessed with the Karen meme. You know, entitled people who are rude when they don't get their own way? He's constantly trying to show us videos with titles like TOP ONE HUNDRED KAREN MOMENTS and THE WORST EVER KARENS IN THE WILD. I don't understand why he finds them so funny.

"And you look like one too," he adds. Which feels a

bit unfair as she can't help it that her name's Karen. For all we know, she could be nice.

"Look like what?" Karen says quietly.

"Say 'I want to speak to your manager'. Go on, please," Jack says.

I nudge Jack and try to warn him to stop talking. He's getting carried away and forgetting himself. But Karen gives me such a *look* that I instantly lose the ability to speak.

"I *am* the duty manager," Karen says. "And right now, I am about ten seconds away from calling the police."

"What have we done?" Emily says, her voice a mixture of indignation and surprise.

"You're really going to call the police?" Jack says, sounding even more delighted. "This is amazing."

Karen doesn't seem to know quite how to respond to this. She huffs in annoyance. "You were seen causing a commotion in the atrium."

"We're sorry," I mumble. I stare so hard at the floor that my eyes threaten to burn holes in the concrete. *Please don't cry*, I plead with myself. My friends will think I'm such a baby if I cry.

Emily kicks my foot and glares at me. "It wasn't us," she says. "Unless you have some actual proof we've done something wrong?"

I can't believe she's talking back to Karen like this. I could never argue with an adult. I feel like all my limbs are turning into jelly. Whereas Emily's staring Karen down like she's not even slightly scared of her.

Karen's face goes very red. She opens and closes her mouth, unsure what to say. "Well ... you shouldn't be here unaccompanied."

Emily laughs. "Unaccompanied? Of course we're not here alone. Our parents are choosing new living-room furniture as we speak."

She folds her arms. "Your parents?"

"Yup. Triplets," Jack says. "Aren't genetics weird?"

She looks between us, clearly trying to work out how we could possibly be related. Then she gives up and points at a sharp bend in the Pink Brick Road leading through into the living-room zone. "I think we should find them, don't you?"

She waits for us to shuffle on ahead and follows us, barking something incomprehensible into her walkie-talkie. "I think we're going to have to make a run for it again," Jack whispers.

"I don't think we should," I say.

"What's the worst that could happen?" Jack says, grinning at me.

I don't get to reply, because Emily points at a group of people about to turn the corner. "Mum! There she is, I can see her."

She takes off at a full sprint. "Wait for us," Jack says, tripping after her. I have no choice but to go with them.

Karen calls for us to stop, but we dart around the corner. The plastic plants all give way to dozens of living rooms. The best part of the Flatpack showroom is the sets. They're these little fake rooms with walls on three sides, decorated with Flatpack products.

The mini living-room sets are laid out in clusters of three or four interconnected rooms. Shelves like you'd find in a normal shop fill the spaces between the sets. They're all stacked high with the cushions, ornaments and the small storage solutions on display in the sets. The bigger pieces of furniture, like sofas and bookcases, have to be ordered using the Flatpack app. By the time a customer makes it through the showroom, their chosen items will be waiting for them in the collection area by the tills.

Thanks to all the high shelves and sets, this zone is a literal maze. Hopefully we'll be able to lose Karen in here. I try to spot somewhere we can hide, but I'm panicking too much to think properly. Jack is also proving to be no help at all. He's holding out his phone, recording himself. "Lads, we're in so much trouble," he pants. "Like and subscribe to find out if I go to prison."

"This way," Emily says, pulling me behind her. The issue with Emily is she's much taller than me and spends nearly *all* of her spare time playing sports. All this running is nothing to her.

I'm not sporty, so running is not nothing. I can already feel my lungs constricting and my legs burning. Although Karen is struggling even more than me. When I glance back at her, she looks pained. She's trying to shout into her walkie-talkie but it's coming out as a series of wheezes.

"We're running, fam," Jack says, the camera shaking

so hard I doubt it's recording anything useful. "Running for our lives."

"Why are you so dramatic?" Emily laughs.

"A Karen wants to kill us," Jack declares. "We're all going to die." His non-stop commentary is doing nothing to make me less terrified.

Emily shoves us both off the Pink Brick Road into one of the sets. "Go, go," she says.

The set has a tropical glamour theme. Fake plants spill from the shelves and there are lots of clashing leaf and flower prints. Emily tries a door at the back of the set, but it's there for decoration and doesn't open. "Oops," she says, shrugging like it's no big deal.

"Get behind the sofa," I cry, feeling like I'm going to pass out from terror.

We crawl out of sight just in time. Karen staggers past our hiding spot. She's making this awful grunting noise that doesn't even sound human. I hold my breath, praying she doesn't see us hiding here. Emily and Jack, however, aren't taking any of this remotely seriously. I can hear them trying to mask their sniggers.

Karen moves on through the zone. I hear her

talking to someone. "Find them," she says. "They're somewhere close by, I know it."

"I think we should give ourselves up," I whisper. "Before things get any worse."

"Don't even think about it," Emily says.

"I'll cry if you do," Jack says. "I swear."

I close my eyes and breathe out slowly. As much as I hate the thought of getting into trouble, saying no to my friends feels impossible. "OK. We need a better hiding place."

I look around for inspiration. Behind the sofa, there's a large dark green dresser. The top half is bookshelves full of hundreds of Flatpack catalogues, ornaments and plastic plants. The bottom half is cupboards. They look big enough for us to climb inside, although it won't be very comfortable. But I don't think we have much choice.

I pull the first one open and, to my surprise, discover the back is open. There's a hole leading into a dark, empty space behind the set.

"Yes!" Emily says. "I think we've found the perfect hiding place."

BEHIND THE SCENES

The hole leads through into darkness. I use my torch to check out our surroundings. We're in a long narrow passageway that runs behind the sets. To my right, there's a flimsy partition separating us from the showroom. To my left, I can reach out and touch the bare metal of the building's outer wall.

It feels like we've found a pocket of dead space hidden behind the cosiness of all the fake living rooms. There's nothing here except some discarded plastic wrap and a few tatty cardboard boxes. Lots of dust. I don't think anyone's been down here for a very long time.

"Do you smell that?" Emily whispers.

I sniff and catch a faint whiff of rotting leaves

and stagnant mud. It reminds me of the woods after months of rain. It reminds me of *that wardrobe* my dads bought from this store. The one that had to be sent back. The one Ada thinks had a monster living in it.

"She who smelt it, dealt it," Jack says, cracking up.

"Nothing alive made that smell," Emily says.

Jack's smile fades. "There better not be a dead animal in here with us."

I think I could cope with something dead. It's living, scuttling, biting things that scare me. Monsters scare me. I tell myself there's no such thing. The smell has to be some kind of stinky mould. Definitely not a sign of a monster infestation.

Only, I'm getting this strange feeling we're being watched.

"Where do you think that leads?" Emily's pointing to a distant door marked WAREHOUSE TWO. When my parents and I returned our wardrobe, the shop worker had it sent to Warehouse Two. I shiver, imagining a whole warehouse full of smelly, potentially haunted furniture.

Jack sets off down the passageway. "We've got some time to explore."

I pull him back. Something tells me we should absolutely not go through that door. "We should stick to the plan," I say quickly. "Focus on pranking Ada and Rube?"

"I suppose that *is* why we're here," Emily agrees.

Jack frowns. I can tell he wants to find out what's in the mysterious Warehouse Two. But then he snaps his attention back to me. He sits down against the wall. "Right. Pranking Ada and Rube. I'm thinking we start small. Scratching noises. The occasional hand shadow puppet. Then when everyone is getting nervous, RARRGH!"

I jump, then shush him. "We're hiding, remember?"

"Maybe we could trap them in a wardrobe or something," he says, dropping his voice to a whisper.

"That would be funny," Emily says.

It doesn't sound funny to me. I'd be terrified if someone shut me in a wardrobe.

"Oh, and so you know, I'm going to go along with being scared when we start doing all the spooky stuff,"

Jack says. "It will make the video funnier, but I won't really be scared."

A quiet scratching sound makes me jump. It's like claws dragging along metal.

Jack startles and throws his arms in the air, then pretends he was fixing his hair. "Perfect, Em. Make noises like that when Rube and Ada are around."

"What?" Emily says. "That wasn't me."

"Ha ha, you're a good liar," he says.

"I'm serious," she says.

The scratching comes again. It brings back horrible memories of that game of flashlight hide-and-seek with Ada. The scuttling noises I was sure Ada made to scare me.

"Em?" Jack clings on to my arm. "Please tell me you're winding us up."

Emily slowly shakes her head. She looks as scared as I feel. My heart bounces around in my chest. The noises are real. There's something in here with us.

Only then, Emily starts to laugh. "You're both so easy to wind up." She drags her nails along the metal wall for us to see. It was a trick. She was messing with us, that's all.

"I knew it was you," Jack says, trying to act casual. "I was playing along, remember?"

"Sure you were." Emily leans back against the partition wall and closes her eyes. How is she relaxed enough to sleep? I'm far too nervous to let down my guard. I can't decide what's scaring me the most – creepy things or getting in trouble.

Jack takes out his phone. "No way, not fair. I've got no reception."

Emily opens one eye. "How will you entertain yourself without TikTok?"

"I have games downloaded," he grumbles. "I don't *need* TikTok; I am just deeply unhappy without it."

For the next hour, Emily dozes and Jack grumpily plays some kind of monster-fighting game on his phone. I spend the whole time worrying about what will happen if we get caught. Eventually, the showroom falls silent and the lights go off. It was already dark in our behind-the-scenes hiding place. Now, it's almost pitch black.

I think about that long passageway leading to the mysterious door marked WAREHOUSE TWO. The door I definitely don't want to go through. It makes me shudder. "Let's get out of here," I say.

We crawl back through the dresser. I check the coast is clear, then emerge into the living-room zone. Most of the lights are off, but I'm relieved to find there are dim security lights every couple of metres. It makes it slightly less scary.

I glance up at the ceiling. There are CCTV cameras watching our every move. "According to Rube's aunt, the security cameras in here aren't monitored and the recordings won't be watched unless something happens. So as long as we don't damage anything or set off the door alarms, no one will ever know we were here," I say, mostly to reassure myself. "The footage is only stored for seventy-two hours and then it's all deleted."

Emily and Jack aren't listening. They're too busy bouncing on a sofa. Jack tries to juggle with three plastic pineapples but ends up dropping them. They noisily bounce across the Pink Brick Road. I pick them up and put them back on a table.

"We have to leave this place *exactly* as we found it," I

say. "Or they'll watch the CCTV recordings tomorrow and we'll be found out."

Emily salutes me, then bursts out laughing. "This is going to be amazing," she says. "Messing around in the showroom. Monster hunting. Pranking those two weirdos."

"Talking of those two weirdos," Jack says. "Where *are* Ada and Rube?"

"I hope they didn't get caught," I say, thinking about how we ditched them and found our own hiding place.

"That would ruin my night," Jack says.

"They'll be hiding somewhere, scared and unable to function alone," Emily says. "Let's find them and have some fun."

THE SCREAM GAME

I shine my torch around the living-room zone. In the half-dark, it is huge and eerie. The criss-cross beams overhead make shadowy patterns on the floor. Abandoned trolleys rest against the walls, part-filled with fake plants and plastic pineapples. Pineapple ornaments are this year's must-have item, according to Dad.

We sneak through the sets, looking behind sofas and checking inside cupboards. I promised myself I would never play flashlight hide-and-seek with Ada again. But here I am, searching for her in the dark.

Jack jumps out from behind a bookcase. "Grrrr," he says. Even though I knew he was there, I still startle.

"Let's play the scream game," Emily says. "Ten points if you can make Ada scream. Two for Rube."

"Rube will be easy," Jack says. "He looks like he'll be a massive coward."

Rube is kind of sensitive. Like that time he hid behind the school shed because of the armadillo documentary. And on our year four bushcraft trip, we found a dead rabbit in the woods and he burst into tears. He cries easily, which sometimes makes me embarrassed for him.

I know it's a horrible thing to think, but I'm glad there's someone here more babyish than me. I imagine Rube's already regretting his choice to come. With the lights out, the store feels huge and menacing. Anything could be hiding around the next corner. I won't be surprised if Rube's already crying.

We arrive at the end of the living-room zone. I peek around a partition into the sofa section of the store. It's a big open area, with row upon row of sofas. They're in every colour, style and fabric. In the middle of the zone, there's a huge four-sided pyramid made of sofas and chairs. There are five steps, each about a metre tall. On each there are sofas and chairs positioned to face outwards, except for the top step, on which there's a lamp.

"It's Mount Doom," Jack jokes. "Do you have the one ring?"

"My precioussssss," Emily hisses.

"It doesn't look very stable," I say.

"We could climb to the top and see if we can spot Ada and Rube," Jack says.

Suddenly, there are footsteps behind us. "What are you kids doing here?" Karen's voice cries. "This is completely unacceptable."

Jack and I scream, but I'm the loudest. I try to run, but in the dark I bump into a sofa. I topple over the back and land on the cushions, where I thrash about like an upturned woodlouse. Then I slide off on to the floor.

Four people lean over me with worried expressions. Jack, Emily, Ada and Rube.

I sit up with a jerk and try to work out where Karen is, but she's nowhere to be seen. "Wh ... what?" I say.

"I am calling the manager right now," Rube says, in an almost perfect impression of Karen's voice. "Oh, I guess I'm the manager, so I am calling me."

Everyone laughs. "That was impressive," Jack says, gently shoving Rube's back. "You sounded exactly like her."

"Can you do other impressions?" Emily says. "I've always wanted to be able to, but I'm rubbish."

"I can only do women," he says. "Little old ladies are my speciality, but Karen has a very distinctive voice that's easy to mimic."

"Hang on, how do you know who Karen is?" Emily says.

"We were hiding, like, two tables away from you," Ada says. "We saw you nearly get yourselves caught."

I swallow heavily and try to remember what we talked about while we hid under that pot plant table. Hopefully nothing mean Ada could get upset about.

"You know what, you're OK," Jack says, putting an arm around Rube's shoulders. "I was worried you'd be boring, but I think tonight's going to be a laugh."

"Right. Thanks, I guess?" Rube says.

A little flicker of shame catches inside me. There I was, presuming Rube would be cowering in terror now the lights have gone out. Instead, he's pranking us and making everyone laugh. If I'm not careful, Emily and Jack will decide they like him better than me.

Jealousy is a horrible emotion, though. At least, that's what Papa tells me. So I try to force a smile on to my face. "Good one," I say. "Really funny."

Rube blinks at me, looking worried. "I didn't mean to scare you," he says.

"I'm fine," I say, laughing. "Don't worry about me."

"How many points do we get for making all of *you* scream?" Ada says.

There's a moment of silence while Jack and Emily realize that she overheard us talking. Then Emily sweeps back her short hair and gives Ada a smug smile. "You'll never make me scream."

The two girls stare each other out. It gets uncomfortable. Neither is going to back down. Rube clears his throat. "Shall we show them what we've been doing?"

Ada shrugs and looks away from Emily. "Sure. Come on." She pulls up her unicorn hood so the bloody horn points the way.

I quickly gather up a cola bottle sweet that's fallen from her pocket – we can't leave any evidence behind – then follow her to the base of Sofa Mount Doom. She's fiddling with a small camera, which she hides behind a cushion on one of the sofas in the pyramid. "We've only got one motion-activated camera. We're going to move it between the zones and see what it records," she explains.

"What's this?" Emily asks, picking up another piece of equipment.

"No, don't touch that!" Rube cries, taking it from her. "I mean, I don't want you to get an electric shock."

"Is all this stuff homemade?" Emily asks.

"I made some modifications," Rube says. "We couldn't afford the real equipment."

"Rube's really talented," Ada says, glaring at me. It's clear she's implying she's traded up when it comes to best friends.

"I, um, wouldn't say that." A blush spreads across Rube's light brown skin. He licks both hands so he can smooth down the severe side parting in his black hair. He manages to look like a forty-year-old accountant and a small eleven-year-old boy at the same time.

"What's this one do?" Jack says, picking up an old rewired analogue radio with a voice recorder duct-taped to the side.

"Um, that's for detecting sound waves outside the human audible range," Rube says. "Other life forms don't always communicate on the same frequencies as us."

"Other life forms? What exactly is it we're looking for?" Emily asks.

"We don't know," Ada sighs. "That's the problem. The shadow we saw at Olive's house was a spider, but none of the Hashtag Haunted Flatpack reviews have mentioned spiders."

"Someone thought they saw a snake," Rube says. "And someone else saw their grandmother's shadow a few weeks after she passed on."

"So a spider-snake-grandma?" Jack says. "That sounds epic."

"My theory is the creatures can change their form, but I have no evidence yet," Ada says.

I cross my arms tightly around my body, like I'm

hugging myself. Monsters that can change their shape is a horrifying thought. Even Emily and Jack look worried. I think that was Ada's intention, as she looks delighted at our expressions.

She throws a cola bottle into her mouth and grins. "All this excitement is making me hungry. Let's pick a base for the evening."

OUR HOUSE

"Welcome to our house," Emily says, putting on a prim and proper voice.

She invites us inside a living-room set full of clashing fabrics. The walls are painted a classy dark blue and there are gold-framed mirrors on the walls. The bookshelves are lined with Flatpack catalogues and unlit candles.

"Do enter, won't you please?" Jack says. He's playing the part of her attentive husband.

He's stuffed a large origami flower into his shirt so it looks like a cravat, and he's wearing a blanket as a cape. Emily has a fake rose in her hair and a string of battery-powered fairy lights round her neck. They've filled cocktail glasses with Jack's blue drinks and he hands one to each of us. I make a mental note to wash the glasses up before we leave.

"What a lovely home you have," Ada says. "You must tell me who your interior designer is."

"Oh my! Your canapé selection is perfection," Rube says, gesturing to the little jars of nuts decorating the coffee table. They're all closed by zip-ties, presumably to stop visitors to the superstore from trying to eat them.

Everyone is so good at pretending to be a grown-up. Everyone except for me. I stand around awkwardly, not sure how to join in. I could compliment Emily on the decor, but Ada's already done that. Besides, I feel too self-conscious. So instead I try to be useful.

"Um, I have a multitool," I say, snipping the cable tie on a jar of cashews. I stuff a handful of nuts into my mouth and chew. At least, I try to chew. The nuts are rock solid and taste disgusting. I think they've been varnished to make them last longer. I quickly spit them out. We can't leave any evidence behind, so I have to tip the nuts into my pocket.

"Dinner tonight will be sandwiches," Emily says.

"Don't ruin your appetite, Olive."

I plonk myself down on the sofa and am swallowed up by a million throw cushions. Dad would love this set. Thinking about him makes me feel homesick. And guilty. I told him I'm staying at Emily's for a sleepover. I've never lied to my parents before and, now we're here, I wish I hadn't done it.

The others all start to eat their sandwiches, but I have no appetite. My tummy is twisting and my head won't stop thinking all these bad thoughts. Like, what if Dad and Papa find out what I've done? Or worse, what if Ada's right and there are monsters in here? What if we all get eaten and our parents never find out what happened to us?

There's a sudden scratching noise and everyone freezes. "What was that?" Emily whispers.

My heart beats faster, but then I notice Jack is filming our reactions and Emily has a sly look on her face. They're pranking us. Emily's probably scratching the side of the sofa.

"I know you're doing that," Ada says wearily.

"Doing what?" Emily says, holding up both hands.

The scratching noise comes again. Everyone glances over at Jack, who tries to look innocent.

"I'm not easy to scare," Ada says. "So bear that in mind for your next prank."

Rube raises a hand. "I am very easy to scare."

Not as easy as me, though. I know Emily and Jack are winding everyone up and I *still* want to run away as fast as I can. We can't run away, though. All the doors in this store are alarmed. We can't leave until tomorrow morning, unless we want to get in a huge amount of trouble.

"I don't think I've *ever* been scared," Emily says, locking stares with Ada. "I don't think it's even possible."

"Maybe that's because you don't have an imagination," Ada says.

"I think you have enough for all of us," Emily replies lightly.

The tension between Ada and Emily is so heavy I can feel it in my throat. When I try to swallow, there's a lump that won't go down. I hate confrontation. Especially when it's my ex-best friend and my current friend squaring up against each other.

"Why don't we play a game?" Ada says. "The last one to scream wins."

"I somehow don't think it will be either of us," Rube whispers to me.

"What's the prize?" Emily says.

"If I win, you come to the leavers' disco wearing an outfit of my choosing," Ada says. "It will be a dress. With murder unicorns on it."

Emily winces, but nods her agreement. "And *when* I win, you come to the disco wearing branded sportswear. Head to toe."

Ada gasps. We all do. Ada doesn't do sportswear, and definitely not brands. "You're not going to win," she says.

"The thing is," Emily says, "I don't believe in monsters, so I know there's literally nothing to be scared of in this place. Good luck making me scream."

Ada sets her drink aside and sits forward in her chair. She drops her voice to a low whisper. "You might not believe in the monsters now, but I can promise you they're here."

Emily laughs. "Don't you think someone would have

seen one of these monsters if they existed?"

"It's a conspiracy," Rube says. "They don't want you to know monsters exist. It might cause panic or something."

"Who is they?" Jack asks.

"The government. Adults. People who like things as they are," Ada says. "Imagine if it came out that everything we thought we knew about the world was wrong. What would happen if creatures that can't be explained by science were proven to be real?"

"I think it would be cool, actually," Jack says.

"You think that because you've got no skin in the game. But what about all the scientists who've built their careers on incorrect theories about what life has to look like? They're not going to accept they're wrong, are they?"

"Scientists are covering it up?" I say, thinking about my aunt Sarah. She's a scientist and she's completely incapable of keeping even the smallest secret. If she knew about the existence of monsters, there is no way she would keep it to herself.

"It's not only the scientists," Ada continues. "It's

governments, and the big corporations who control the governments. Imagine there are life forms living in people's wardrobes. Don't you think those life forms deserve the same rights you and I have? That would mean a whole lot of hassle and expense for companies like Flatpack. They would have to consider the welfare of the creatures. They wouldn't want that, would they?"

"People would demand change," Rube says. "There'd be protestors outside Flatpack's doors, campaigning for the creatures' protection."

"Others would probably come here with guns, wanting to hunt them down and put them in a museum," Emily says.

Ada and Rube both give her a horrified look.

She holds up her hands. "Just saying. You reveal the existence of monsters to the world and it's not only the good people who'll pay attention."

Rube looks crestfallen. "I hadn't thought about that."

"It isn't the important part," Ada says.

"What is the important part?" I ask.

"The truth, of course! It's not right that we're all treated like fools who will mindlessly believe everything we're spoon-fed by *The Man*. Proving the existence of these creatures could open the door for governments to admit the existence of other life forms, like Bigfoot and the Loch Ness Monster, and aliens."

"Aliens totally do exist," Jack says. "My aunt Moira was abducted once."

"The aunt Moira who believes there are alligators in the sewers?" Emily says.

"There *are* alligators in the sewers," Ada says.

Emily, Jack and I exchange looks.

"They're cute when they're small." Ada tilts her head like she's thinking. "So people decide they'll make good pets. But then they start to bite."

"Their owners flush them down the toilet," Rube says, his voice hitching like he might cry. "Humans can be so cruel."

"Worse, though – the flushed alligators don't die in the sewers. They get hungrier and hungrier until one day, you're sitting on the toilet and SNAP!" Ada jerks forward and claps her hands together. I jump and throw most of my blue drink in the air. Now I'm going to have to scrub the carpet to make sure we don't leave behind a stain.

Ada cracks up laughing. "Your faces are all great."

Our conversation is interrupted by a loud buzzing noise that reminds me of a giant wasp. Already on edge from Ada's story, I shriek and throw the rest of my drink in my own face. When I compose myself and wipe blue liquid from my eyes, everyone is staring at me.

Rube holds up a pager. "Sorry, just me."

"Something's triggered the motion-activated camera," Ada says, wrapping up her half-eaten sandwiches. "Let's go see what we've caught."

GIVE ME YOUR HAND

We creep through the living-room zone, back into the sofa section. Rube goes first, holding up a weird-looking device. It emits a clicking noise as a needle flicks across the dial. The clicking intensifies as we walk along the rows of sofas and chairs.

"What's that measuring?" I ask.

"Fluctuations in the magnetic field," he says. "It can be a sign of non-traditional life forms."

Non-traditional. I find myself wondering what the monsters would look like, if they were real of course. Spider-ish, probably. Spiders are my worst creature in the whole world. They disgust me on every level. The weird eyes, the hairiness, the unpredictable scuttling.

As I think this, a literal scuttling noise makes us all jump. It could be legs on concrete. Long, bendy, spidery legs. It could also be Emily's fingernails tapping against a coffee table. I want to believe it's the second option, but I can't be sure.

"There's something in here," Emily whispers, her voice shaky.

Too dramatic. Emily doesn't do dramatic, which means it was definitely her making the noise.

"Oh please," Ada says. "Try harder."

"I don't know what you're talking about," Emily says innocently.

Rube's device clicks faster and faster. We come to a bottleneck in the sofas and Ada gestures for Emily to go first. "Unless you're too scared?"

"Of course I'm not scared," Emily says. "But if it makes you feel better if I lead then that's fine."

She marches ahead quickly, with Ada keeping pace. They jostle to be the one in front.

"They remind me of spotted hyenas," Rube says. "Their communities are matriarchal and the female hyenas will fight for dominance."

"You're in trouble if either of them hears you comparing them to the ugliest animal in the world," Jack says.

Rube looks horrified. "But hyenas are beautiful. Not that I think ... Ada and Emily... I mean..."

Jack squeezes his shoulders in a quick massage. "Stop digging, my friend."

Ada glances back at us. "Can you all hurry up, please?"

As we catch up, there's another scuttling noise. It has to be Emily pranking us. I hope it's Emily. But a little voice in my head worries that this time it isn't.

"We're safe, right?" Jack says. "I mean, these creatures don't eat people, do they?"

Ada and Rube exchange looks. Neither of them speaks.

"They *eat* people?" Jack says, more loudly.

"*Shush,*" Ada says. "You'll scare it away."

There's another scuttling noise. I'm reminded of a wildlife documentary in which a pack of predators slowly circle their prey. Sneaking closer and closer, then pouncing once there's nowhere left to run.

"I'm going to be eaten, aren't I?" Jack sighs.

"Nothing would want to eat you. You'd taste disgusting," Emily says.

"Er, *excuse* me?"

"That body spray you're wearing is enough to repel even the meanest of human-eating creatures," she says.

"Well, you'd be chewy," Jack says. "You have too many muscles."

"Ha. Like anything would dare try to eat me. I'd punch it in the face."

Emily and Jack's good-natured argument is silenced by another burst of the scraping, scratching sound. It hits me that they can't be the ones making the noises. Rube's device clicks so fast it becomes one long warning tone.

"Full disclosure," Ada says. "A man went missing in this shop and he was never found."

"What?" I say.

Ada pauses and leans back against one of the sofa beds, sighing dramatically. "There was a store worker. Marcus Knight. Here, I have a photo."

She takes out her phone and shows me a picture.

Marcus has the sort of face you expect to see on a police mugshot. He's in his forties or fifties, with a nose that looks like it's taken a lot of punches and the angriest eyes I've ever seen. His mouth is slightly open in a snarl, revealing a gold tooth.

"He worked here?" Emily says. "Wow."

"Behind the scenes," Rube says. "His face doesn't scream customer service, does it? Like, imagine asking him to help you pick out new curtains."

"I know it's a photo, but I'm genuinely scared he's going to leap out through the phone screen and try to strangle me," Jack says.

They have a point. Marcus is totally the sort of person you could imagine having a serial-killer nickname. Like the Flatpack Hacker or Marcus "Knifey" Knight.

"Marcus worked in the warehouse," Ada continues. "He was here for eight years. Then, one day, he vanished."

"Vanished?" I say, gulping.

"He clocked in for his shift early one morning. He kept to himself, so no one knows exactly when he disappeared. All we know is he never clocked out. His coat and car keys were found in his locker. His car was still in the car park."

"Maybe he walked out the front door and decided to reinvent himself somewhere new," Jack says hopefully. "People fake their own deaths all the time."

"Do they?" I say.

"My cousin Millie did," Rube says. "She had all these debts, so she staged a drowning accident at sea. Then she moved back in with my aunt but wore a wig and glasses when she went outside. She honestly thought people wouldn't notice."

"You're getting off topic," Ada says. "Marcus didn't fake his own death. He's still here. In this building."

"How would that work?" I say. "Surely someone would have noticed."

"It's a big store," Rube says. "Plenty of dark places where someone could get lost. Forever."

"Get lost or get eaten?" Jack says. "Because there's a difference."

"My theory?" Ada says, lowering her voice in the same way she does when she's telling a ghost story. "He was dragged into a wardrobe by one of the creatures, never to be seen again."

"My theory is the wardrobes lead to their shadow realm," Rube says mysteriously. "That's probably where they ate him."

I laugh abruptly. *Shadow realm*? "OK, that sounds silly. Right?" I look at everyone else, hoping someone will back me up. Emily does this little shrug thing and stays silent.

"Let's keep moving," Ada says, clearly pleased with herself.

We continue walking. My feet feel heavy. My ears are on high alert for scuttling sounds. We turn a corner and reach the sofa pyramid. It takes a second for me to realize the sofa where Ada hid her camera is … gone. There's now an empty space on the bottom row.

"How can an entire sofa vanish?" Jack whispers.

We all stare at the pyramid. There's a big gap where the sofa used to be, making a doorway to the hollow centre of the pyramid. It's dirty in the middle – full of dust and bits of bubble wrap.

Emily grins at us. "This pyramid is taller than the walls separating all the zones, right?"

"I like what you're thinking," Jack says. "Race you to the top."

"Wait, what?" I say. "No, that's not safe!"

Ada and Rube climb after the other two. "The view will be good," Ada says. "We might spot something in one of the other zones."

They leave me standing on the ground in disbelief. I can't believe they're doing something so dangerous, for no good reason at all. I suspect they only want to climb the pyramid because they know they're not allowed to.

"I can see so much," Rube says. "This must be what it feels like to be a bird."

"I can't see the missing sofa, though," Ada says.

I hear something behind me. A scratching, scraping sound again. It came from under a nearby sofa bed. I look up at the pyramid. Emily and Jack are right at the top. It can't have been them making the noise. So what was it?

I nervously circle the sofa bed, looking for the source of the noise. I bend down and check underneath, shining my torch into the darkness. Something moves.

I don't know what it is and I'm not sticking around long enough to find out.

"Wait for me," I cry, running for the others. I climb on to the first step of the sofa pyramid. "I saw something," I say.

"Saw what?" Ada pauses on the third step and looks down at me.

"I don't know! But there's something in here with us." I clamber up to the next level. My limbs are already shaky at being so high off the ground.

"Good one," Jack says, laughing. His smile fades. "What do you mean, there's something in here with us?"

I try to scramble on to the third step of the pyramid. My foot slips on one of the scaffolding poles supporting the structure. I drop straight through a gap between the sofas. I barely manage to grab the leg of a sofa to stop myself from falling. I cry out and the metal scaffold clangs loudly as my feet kick against it.

I glance down. The floor looks like it's miles away. But the concrete isn't the part I'm most concerned about. It's the shifting shadows that swirl beneath me.

They remind me of churning lava, or maybe that's my imagination. Jack did describe this sofa pyramid as Mount Doom, after all. My mind has turned it into a towering volcano. I'm dangling over the Cracks of Doom, about to be disintegrated like the One Ring.

Jack reaches through a gap from the step above me. "Take my hand," he says.

"My fingers are slipping!" I cry. "Don't let me fall."

"See if you can pull yourself back up," Emily says. "I can't get to you."

"I can't hold on. I can't—" My sweaty fingers lose their grip and I fall. I've barely started to scream when I hit the ground. My knees jar. Dust billows up from the floor.

"Olive, are you OK?" Rube shouts.

I brush myself down. "Yeah, I'm fine," I say sheepishly. "It wasn't a very big drop."

Now I'm down here, there are no shadows. I think I imagined them in my panic. What there is, is a camera. I hold it up for the others to see.

"Cameron!" Rube cries in delight. "You're OK!"

Everyone climbs down to join me and we huddle in a circle. There's one twenty-second clip saved in the camera's memory. We lean in closer as Ada hits play. The clip is of the sofa zone, still and silent. I can't help but feel relieved there's nothing else in the shot.

My relief lasts seconds. Something huge and hairy moves across the screen. Without anything else to go on, my mind fills in the blanks. I imagine a furry octopus, with thick white tentacles. A mouth that can swallow a person whole.

I gasp and stumble back from the camera. No one else is bothered, though. "Is that an arm?" Emily says.

Ada angles the camera and squints. "Yeah, it is," she says, sounding disappointed. "It's one of those twin Flatpack workers."

I can see it now. It's not a tentacle. I'm not sure why I thought it was.

"Is there sound?" Jack says.

"Hang on, I'll restart the clip," Ada says. This time she turns up the volume.

"The Bridgeton in vibrant lime," Karen's voice says.

"This is the sofa we need."

"But it's heavy and I'm tired," one of the twins whines in their high-pitched voice.

"Whose fault is that?" Karen's voice replies. "If you'd noticed there weren't any left in the warehouse, we wouldn't have to take this one."

"Stock's not our responsibility," the twins say in unison.

Ada sighs. "Karen and her minions must be finishing up tomorrow's delivery orders before going to the

party. Just our luck the sofa they needed had our camera balanced on it."

"At least they didn't see the camera," Rube says.

On the clip, there are pained grunting noises as the sofa is dragged out of the pyramid. The camera image shakes.

"Careful," Karen snaps. "Come on then, let's get it to the lift."

A big hairy arm reaches in front of the camera and the sofa is lifted from the ground. "How are we going to explain where it's gone?" one of the twins says. "People will notice the gap."

"That's easy. We'll say it smelt funny, so we stored it in Warehouse Two," Karen says. The twins both laugh.

"No one will question it," one of the men says. "They're terrified the bad smell is going to spread to more furniture."

"It's such a clever plan. We say stock is damaged and then we sell it ourselves and keep the money," the second twin adds.

"It could be me," Rube whispers, "but I don't think they're preparing an order for delivery."

The camera's shot bobs up and down as the twins try to get a better grip on the sofa. Then all of a sudden, the image somersaults through the air. The camera hits the ground and the recording stops.

"This clip isn't evidence of a monster," Ada says sadly. "It's evidence of theft."

THE THIEVES

We follow the Pink Brick Road into the dining-room zone.

"We're off to see the lizard," the others sing, skipping arm in arm. I skulk behind them, arms folded and brow furrowed.

"Look, I'm the tin man," Jack says, putting a metal wastepaper basket on his head.

Everyone else laughs, but I can feel myself getting more and more frustrated. "We're supposed to be looking for somewhere to have a meeting," I say, earning myself four confused stares. "To discuss our options?"

"What we need is a big, serious, grown-up table,"

Ada says, putting on a silly voice. "So we can have a big, serious, grown-up meeting."

"Oh fine," Emily sighs. "Over here."

She leads us into a pineapple-themed set with a shiny pink table. Everything is pineapple, from the wallpaper to the cushions to the paintings on the walls. To top it off, there are little pineapple models balanced on every surface like an invading army. Dad would love it in here. I try to stop thinking about him.

"I'm actually allergic to pineapples," Jack says. "This room is a lot."

"That's a weird thing to be allergic to," Emily says, unwrapping her half-eaten sandwich. "What do you have on pizza if you can't have pineapple?"

"Um, the same as every other *normal* person in the world. Anything except for pineapple."

"He has a point," Ada says, adding a handful of cola bottles to her cheese sandwich and squashing it flat. "Only a weirdo has pineapple on their pizza."

"You know what's good on pizza?" Rube says. "Vegan tuna."

The table erupts with a chorus of nos. Everyone

laughs, except for me. I'm the only one not joining in with the jokes. I'm the only one sitting in front of an empty plate. I can't laugh. I can't eat. I'm too worried.

"What are we going to do?" I blurt out.

Everyone stops their conversation and looks over at me. "What do you mean?" Emily says.

I gesture back at the sofa section, alarmed that she's already forgotten. "Karen and the twins are still in the store?"

"It doesn't change anything," Ada says through a mouthful of her sandwich.

"It kind of does," I snap. "If they'd come into the living-room zone while we were there, they would have caught us."

"They didn't, though. And from the sound of things, they've gone back down to the warehouse," Ada says. "They only came up here to get that sofa."

Jack puts up his hand. "Why are they here? I'm confused about that part."

"The simplest explanation is they're stealing stock and selling it on the black market," Rube says.

"Is there a black market for stolen Flatpack

products?" Emily says. "It can't be that profitable."

"That part isn't important," I say, starting to get exasperated. "What matters is how much trouble we'll be in if they come back up here."

"Even if we wanted to leave, we can't," Rube says. "The doors are alarmed."

"If we set off the alarms, they'll look at the CCTV." Jack blows one of the store's cameras a kiss. "I will be in so much trouble if my parents find out about this."

"So, we either spend the whole night hiding on the off chance Karen and the twins come back upstairs, or we carry on with the original plan," Ada says. "I know what my choice is."

"Hiding?" I say hopefully.

Everyone looks at me and bursts out laughing.

"You're funny," Jack says.

"We're going to continue moving along the Pink Brick Road, looking for the creatures in each zone," Ada says.

"But what about—" I start to say. Only then I spot movement at the entrance to the dining-room zone. "Karen's here," I whisper.

"Everyone hide," Ada orders. She runs out of the pineapple dining-room and ducks behind a display cabinet full of cutlery. Jack and Emily cocoon themselves in the set's heavy velvet curtains. It looks like it's every kid for themselves.

Rube and I stand there, unsure where to go. "Quick, in that cupboard," he whispers.

"Wait!" I quickly gather up everyone's food from the table and toss it into a basket of hessian place mats, hoping Karen and the twins won't notice.

Then I cram myself into the cupboard with Rube and we pull the door closed just in time. Karen stops metres away from our hiding place. I can see her through a crack between the badly made doors. "Cola bottles," she says. "I can smell cola bottles."

"Ada," Rube whispers.

"It's those kids from earlier," Karen says.

"Why would they still be here?" one of the twins replies.

"Because they're troublemakers," Karen says.

"We can check the security footage," the other one says. "Find out where they're hiding."

Karen turns to him, hands on her hips. "I hope the cameras aren't recording, because that would interfere with our plans."

"Oh yeah," he says, laughing nervously.

"Please tell me you did turn them off. Because I don't want anyone to find out what we're doing here tonight, do you?"

"No, I definitely did it. Don't worry about it."

I briefly feel a sense of relief that nothing we've got up to tonight has been caught on camera. Then I start to worry that, if anything does happen to us, there will be no evidence.

"Do you think she asked for hair like that?" Rube whispers in my ear. "Stripes are a bold choice if you're not a numbat."

I snap out of worrying about the cameras. "A what?"

"Numbat. It's an Australian marsupial. Looks like a cute stripy squirrel, but they've got long tongues because they eat termites."

Karen's hair does look like a small animal has crawled on to her head and died. It has a fur-like quality, with tufty bits at the back and a long sweeping slab of hair hanging over one eye. I stifle a laugh, then clamp a hand over my mouth.

Karen turns and I think she's heard me. But then she stamps her foot in a huff. "Make sure there are no kids in the store. Do it now!"

"OK, OK. We'll look," a twin says, his voice soothing.

"Everywhere," Karen says.

"Yeah, totally. No cushion will go unturned."

Karen huffs again and marches off, leaving the two men looking grumpy. "Let's get a cup of tea then tell her we swept the whole building and found nothing," one says.

"What if there are kids still here?"

"Why would there be kids here?"

The man shrugs. "I don't know. But I don't want to get on Karen's bad side."

The first man sighs heavily. "That implies she has a good side."

"One lap of the showroom and then we get some tea, OK?"

"Sounds fair, bro." They high-five each other.

They head in our direction. I can see them checking underneath tables and looking in cupboards. My heart rate doubles. There's nowhere for us to go. If they look in our set, we'll be caught. I'm not sure that's such a bad thing, to be honest. At least we'd get to go home. But I still can't help but feel a sense of dread as they come closer and closer.

Rube wrinkles his nose. "Olive, is that you?"

"Is what me?"

"The horrific smell!"

The smell wasn't there a moment ago, but now our hiding place reminds me of the depths of the woods after months of rain. Rotting leaves and stagnant mud. "Of course it's not me," I whisper.

"Is it a skunk?" he says. "I'd love to meet a skunk; they're fascinating creatures."

I shake my head, unable to speak. I don't think we're alone in this cupboard, not any more. I can sense a presence. Something hiding in the darkness.

The twins stop right outside. They're inches away from us.

"Do you want a mint?" one of them says, taking

something out of his pocket. "Your breath smells terrible."

"What? It's not my breath. It's your armpits!"

"They can smell it too," Rube whispers, right against my ear.

The smell's getting stronger. All the hairs on the back of my neck prickle. I *know* there's something watching me through the darkness, poised to strike. I can't speak, I can't move, I can't breathe.

One of the twins puts his nose up to the crack between the doors. He sniffs. "I think it's this cupboard," he says.

"Another one for Warehouse Two," his colleague grumbles. "Let's leave it for the morning crew."

They move on. I wait until their voices have faded before I shove the doors open, toppling out on to the rug. Rube stands over me, looking confused. When I look, the cupboard is completely empty.

ALL IN MY IMAGINATION

I'm so embarrassed. I need to hold it together. I'm so not holding it together. Emily and Jack don't even need to try to prank me. My brain is pranking itself, making me see things that aren't there. Hear noises that aren't real.

"Was there something in the cupboard with us?" Rube says.

I shake my head. "No. I … I got carried away, that's all."

"Why are you lying?" Ada says, stomping over. Her rainbow tail swishes angrily. "You saw the monster again, didn't you?"

Emily and Jack step out from behind their curtains.

They're looking at me with such pity.

"I didn't see anything," I say. "There's nothing to see. Because monsters don't exist!"

That's when the scratching noise starts again.

"Stop it!" I shout at Emily. "I've had enough of the pranks, OK? I've had enough!"

She holds up both hands. "Olive, that's not me."

The scratching comes again, this time closer.

"It's not me either," Jack says. "Honest."

The whole group exchanges looks. *Scratch, scritch, scrabble*, goes the noise.

"If none of us are doing that, then what is?" Rube whispers.

Everything goes very quiet for a moment. In a nearby set, a curtain billows. There's something hiding behind it. Claws scratch against the floor. We all huddle together in a group and slowly back away along the Pink Brick Road. My torch shakes in my hand as I lift the beam to shine on the curtains.

A huge shadow rises up the wall. It's like a really, really big lizard. It has a long, rounded snout and protruding eyes. A long neck and short arms with vicious claws. I've seen enough dinosaur films to know exactly what it is – a velociraptor.

"It's not real. It's a hallucination," I say. I'm imagining it and maybe if I close my eyes, it will disappear.

"I can see it too," Rube says.

"We can all see it," Emily says.

The raptor's shadow prowls towards us, sliding across the walls. It makes it scarier that I can't see the actual dinosaur, only its shadow. The dinosaur itself is somehow managing to hide itself from view, camouflaged like it's stalking us through the jungles of Isla Nublar.

"I think we should…" Jack whispers. "I think we … we should…"

"Run!" Emily shouts, as the shadow drops on to its haunches and prepares to pounce.

I don't need to be told twice. We all take off through the dining-room zone, following the twists and turns of the Pink Brick Road. The shadow keeps pace with us. One moment, it's moving along a partition wall. The next, it's somehow jumped to the opposite side of the showroom and is sliding over a wooden sideboard.

It's sticking to the edges of the room, I realize. The Pink Brick Road takes a more direct route. We can outrun it. Then Jack trips over a large basket full of yet more plastic pineapples. The basket crashes to the ground and all the pineapples skitter across the floor. Jack rolls over the upended basket and lands on one of the pineapples, yelping when its spiky leaves poke him in the belly.

"You're the clumsiest person ever," Emily says, heaving him upright by his jacket.

"Watch the velvet," he complains, now limping as he runs.

We weave through shelves selling all the small items showcased in the dining-room sets. I spot place mats, candlesticks and tablecloths. We fight our way through a set full of more fake plastic plants and find ourselves in the next zone: kitchens. Claws scratch at the floor behind us, faster and faster, closer and closer.

"In here," Emily says, pulling me off the Pink Brick Road and into one of the kitchen sets.

The whole kitchen is chrome. The oven, the doors,

the work surfaces. It reminds me of my school kitchen. It even has the same ugly metal shelves. We all duck down behind the central island, huddling together. I can see our distorted reflections in the cupboard doors. My face is sweaty and terrified.

We wait, but I can't hear anything. Jack peeks out from behind the island then ducks back out of sight again. "There's still something out there."

"What sort of something?" Emily asks.

"I don't know! Something big," he answers.

"It's clearly a dinosaur," Ada hisses.

"Dinosaurs are extinct!" Emily says.

The scratching starts up again. In the shiny cupboards across from our hiding place, I can see a dark shape moving our way. I've seen this film. I know the dinosaur is hunting us.

"What's weird is the lack of feathers," Rube says curiously. "It's commonly believed raptors were closer to modern-day birds than reptiles."

"Is now the time?" Jack whispers.

Rube shrugs. "It makes me wonder what's *really* out there."

"What do you mean?" Emily says, but Ada shushes her.

The scratching sound gets closer. I risk a brief glance around the corner. The low lighting in the showroom reflects in all the chrome. A shadow passes across one of the doors. It's big. Really big.

"It's coming this way," I say, my voice shaking.

As quietly as possible, we crawl from behind the central island and hide behind a tall shelving unit. Through the gaps between pots and pans, I can see the shadow's distorted reflection in the metal units.

"We're going to have to make a run for it," Ada says.

We slowly rise to our feet. But Jack bumps into a hanging display of kitchen utensils. They clatter loudly and a ladle falls to the ground. I see the shadow stop, then turn its head towards the noise.

"Go," Emily whispers. "Now!"

We scramble out from behind the shelving unit and run. I risk a glance back and that's when I realize Jack's not with us. He's sitting frozen against one of the cupboards, his eyes wide.

I skid to a halt. "Come on," I plead, but he shakes his head. I think he's too scared to move.

I can't see the shadow now. It's worse not knowing where it is. It could be anywhere.

A loud crash makes me shudder. Emily is bashing two pans together in a nearby kitchen set. "You want to eat me?" she shouts. "Come on then!"

The shadow rises up the wall of her set. She drops the pans and runs. It strikes me that I still haven't seen the actual dinosaur. Only its silhouette on the walls. There's not much light in here, sure. But I don't understand why I can't see the dinosaur.

I grab Jack's hand. "We need to go," I say.

"Yeah. Good idea," he says.

We run hand-in-hand through the kitchen sets. There are so many of them. An old-fashioned country kitchen. A sleek modern kitchen. White cupboards and black marble. There are shelves of pots, pans and utensils. Rows of ovens and dishwashers lined up for customers to choose from.

We race down the aisles of products and finally I spot the next zone ahead. It's bathrooms. Before we can get there, a shadow rises to block our way. It slides across a tiled wall.

"It's got ahead of us!" I cry.

We're forced to changed direction. Our only option is a narrow path half-hidden behind one of the kitchen sets. It's one of the store's secret shortcuts. We burst out into the first zone, full of plastic houseplants. The shortcut has taken us back to the start of the showroom. The others are here already.

"Run for the exit!" Emily shouts over her shoulder. "Get out of here."

We push our way through the plants, knocking them off shelves and not caring about the mess. I can hear the monster chasing us. Its razor-sharp claws scrabble on the floor. It crashes into shelves. I don't dare look back.

We race out of the showroom. The atrium is eerie in the dark. The escalators are still and silent. I want to run downstairs and burst out of the front doors, into the cold night air. But I already know the doors are locked. There's nowhere for us to run, so we do the next best thing and we hide.

"The canteen's through here," Jack cries.

We trip over chairs in our panic. The tables are all tightly packed to cram as many people in as possible. At the end of the canteen, there's a doorway leading to the lifts down to the collection area and the tills. But we don't have time to go that way.

Instead, we run towards the canteen kitchen. We throw ourselves over the shiny serving counter and plop down on to the tiled floor. The kitchen is dark and smells of cleaning products. Emily drags the hatch closed and we sit in a huddle. I move my torch between the door and the hatch.

"We're safe in here, right?" Jack says.

"Yes, unless they figure out how to open doors," Ada replies.

Right then the door handle rattles. I scream.

MEATPOP REGRET

The handle rattles again. Jack and I cling on to each other as the door slowly opens. A figure stands silhouetted against the moonlit canteen. It doesn't have teeth and claws. Instead, it's about the size of an eleven-year-old carrying a massive backpack.

"You left me behind," Rube says.

"Quick, get inside," Emily says, pulling him into the kitchen and shutting the door behind him.

Ada flips on the kitchen lights. They're glaringly bright after all the darkness in the showroom.

"You all ran off and didn't wait for me," Rube says indignantly.

"You were right with us!" Jack says.

"I got tangled in a plant. I can't believe you left me! I was calling out for help and everything."

"Sorry, but we were being chased by a velociraptor," Emily says. "It's everyone for themselves when velociraptors are involved."

"Velociraptors were actually the size of turkeys," Rube says sulkily. "I think that was closer to the size of a utahraptor."

"A *dinosaur* chased us!" Jack says. "I thought the monsters were supposed to be spiders. I was OK with spiders, but not dinosaurs."

"The shadow of a dinosaur chased us," I say quietly.

"What?" Emily says, looking straight at me.

"Did any of you see an actual dinosaur? Because I didn't."

Ada seems to consider this. "It is strange, now you mention it. When I was going through the haunted Flatpack reviews online, I noticed no one has ever reported seeing an actual monster. It's only ever shadows."

"No one's mentioned a utahraptor shadow before," Rube says.

Ada gets out her notebook and flicks through the pages. "You're right. Someone reported a werewolf and someone else saw the shadow of a grizzly bear on his bedroom wall. No dinosaurs."

Jack abruptly claps his hands together. "I don't know about all of you, but this has given me an appetite." He starts digging around in one of the industrial-sized fridges. We were all almost eaten mere seconds ago and he's thinking about his stomach.

"Did anyone get any footage?" Ada asks.

"I was too busy running for my life," Jack says. "Sorry."

"Same," Rube says.

"That's frustrating, but next time we'll be better prepared," Ada says. "Jack, I'm promoting you to official videographer and—"

"Wait, what?" I cry. "What do you mean, *next time*?"

"We need real evidence, Olive," Ada says. "This is why we came here."

I open and close my mouth. This is ridiculous. She's being ridiculous! How can Ada be thinking about evidence, and Jack be thinking about food at a time like this? I'm so frustrated I could scream, but I've done enough of that and I don't want to give our hiding place away to either the dinosaur or to Karen and the twins.

"Aha!" Jack cries, emerging from the fridge. He's holding a vacuum-packed bag of meatpops. They look even more hideous than usual, all squished together in one big lump. He tries to tear into the bag with his teeth. When he can't, he goes in search of a pair of scissors.

"We'll need weapons," Emily says. "I'm not going anywhere near a velociraptor without at least a long stick I can poke it with."

"Utahraptor," Rube says. "But I agree."

"What?" I say in disbelief.

"I'm in, lads," Jacks says, holding the open bag up in the air. "Behold!"

He accidentally tips the bag, sending meatpops all over the floor. They bounce, which doesn't strike me as normal. Meat shouldn't bounce. He gathers most of them up and shoves a handful into the closest microwave. It has a setting specifically for meatpops. It lights up and makes a quiet whirring noise as they cook.

"How do we fight off a shadow?" Emily says.

"A bright light?" Rube replies.

"We should make ourselves unwieldy," Ada says.

"Unwieldy?" I whisper.

"Yeah. A few throw cushions under our tops so it's hard to drag us away. They'll be good bite protection too."

I stare at them all, open-mouthed. They're talking about going back into the showroom to look for the creature that tried to attack us. It makes no sense.

"The most important part is we film everything," Ada continues. "Jack, if you can—"

"This is ridiculous!" I cry, silencing Ada. "We need to get out of here. We need to go home!"

"No way. Our parents will be furious," Emily says.

"And we can't leave the store," Rube says. "It's already dark outside, and cold."

"Then we should hide right here until the morning!"

"That sounds boring," Ada says, looking around the kitchen and shuddering.

"What about Karen, hmm?" I say. "She's looking for us, remember?"

"That's a good point," Rube says.

"We can set up motion sensors around the entrances and exits into and out of the showroom. If they go off, we hide. Simple," Ada says, shrugging.

I make a choked cry of exasperation. No one is listening to me.

The microwave pings. "Snack time!" Jack cries. He places the meatpops into a cup he's found and brings them over. "Help yourselves."

Rube pulls a face. "I'm a vegetarian. But thanks."

Jack grabs one, blowing on it as steam rises into the air. "I've never tried a meatpop. This is a big day for me."

"It looks kind of ... wrong," Rube says. "Do you even know what's in it?"

"Meat," Jack says.

"That's not strictly accurate," I snap, still angry that all my sensible suggestions are being ignored. "I believe the ingredients list specifies *animal parts*."

Jack pulls a face, then checks the list on the bag. "What parts?" he whispers.

"They're seventy-five pence," I say. "Take a guess."

He narrows his eyes at the meatpop, then takes a small bite. "Interesting, interesting," he says. "Slightly grainy, but the flavour's there."

"Seriously?" I say. "What is wrong with you?"

Jack holds my stare and sucks the rest of the meatpop off the stick in one huge gulp. Then he makes a pained huffing noise when he finds out how hot it is.

"You've not paid for them," I say, knowing that I sound like a complaining old lady, but that doesn't stop me.

Jack smacks his lips together. He manages to swallow his meatpop and shudders. He hands me the stick. "You know, I think I made a mistake."

"This whole thing is a mistake! We should never have come here."

Obviously, no one listens to me.

INTO BATTLE

Jack has a colander on his head, Rube has armed himself with a long pair of tongs and Emily is wielding a saucepan like a bat. Ada is wearing oven gloves for no good reason at all.

"Here's the plan," Ada says. "We're going to sneak through the houseplant zone into living rooms, where we'll make our base camp."

"Living rooms will be safe," Emily says. "We were in there for ages earlier."

This makes no sense, but I don't bother trying to argue. Instead, I sit there with my arms folded and a scowl on my face.

"After we've put on our cushion armour, we'll take

the secret shortcut through to kitchens." Ada tries to show us the route on a Flatpack map, but her oven gloves get in the way.

"The dinosaur will be in kitchens?" Jack says.

"Totally," Ada says. "I'm sure of it."

"How can you be sure?" I say, crossing my arms. "How?"

No one can answer me, so they ignore the question.

"I need to place the anti-Karen motion sensors before we do anything," Rube says. "There are only three ways in and out of the showroom – the entrance, the exit and a staff lift and stairwell in sofas. Once we have the sensors in place, I'll get paged if anyone comes into the showroom."

"What if they're already in there, looking for us?" I say.

"Stop being so argumentative. And they won't still be there," Ada says. "It's been ages. They'll have given up by now."

"You're sure of that too?" I say.

"Yes, I'm sure," Ada says, glaring at me.

"Those twins weren't exactly enthusiastic about

trying to find us, were they?" Jack says. "They're probably drinking tea downstairs by now."

I roll my eyes. This plan involves a lot of presumptions. I don't like to presume anything.

"All right," Emily says. "Let's get this show on the road."

Reluctantly, I follow the others out of the kitchen and into the moonlit canteen. Rube goes to set up his sensor at the exit from the showroom. Emily goes in the opposite direction to check that the entrance into the houseplant zone is clear.

While the rest of us wait, I stare out at the dark car park. There are a few cars littered beneath street lamps. In the distance, I can make out the town. The walk is about a mile, which isn't far when it's light out. In the dark, it's a forever away.

Emily returns and waves at us. "Come on, the coast's clear."

"What about Rube?" I say.

"I'm here," he says, tapping me on the shoulder and making me jump.

We sneak into the houseplant zone, sticking

together with Emily taking the lead. Everything is silent. We check behind every shelf and every display, but there's no sign of either Karen and the twins, or the dinosaur.

I pick up the products we knocked over on the way through and put them back where they belong. We don't want anyone realizing we've been through here. I'm setting a spider plant on a shelf when I hear something rustle. I freeze and crane my ears to listen for another noise. I don't hear anything, though.

It's a relief to get to the living-room zone. We set up our base of operations in a living room themed like a jungle. It's full of more plastic houseplants, obviously. There are also lots of leaf-print fabrics and statues of animals.

Rube sets off to put his final sensor outside the staff lifts in sofas, while the others get ready to take on the monster. Emily finds a roll of duct tape and they tape cushions to their backs and tummies. Jack also puts on a curtain as a cape, which seems completely unnecessary to me.

"From a physics perspective, capes are a danger,"

I mutter from my position on the sofa. "They can get caught in things."

"But they're also awesome," he says, swishing it in my face. "Let's look for more weapons."

"What about this table lamp?" Emily tosses her saucepan aside and picks up a tree-shaped lamp. She tests its weight in her hand. "I could get a good swing with this thing."

"These pineapples look like grenades," Jack says, filling his pockets.

I close my eyes. I'm going to be eaten. The others aren't taking this half as seriously as they should be. They're all ... having fun! I listen in as they argue about what a raptor's biggest weakness is. They're forgetting the thing stalking us isn't even a *real* raptor. Whatever it is, I doubt it's something we can fight off with plastic pineapples and a saucepan.

"So, to recap," Jack says, "if we're attacked, we're going to throw meatpops to distract it. Then I'll pelt it with pineapple grenades and Emily will hit it in the kneecaps?"

Emily slaps her lamp against her palm. "Bring it on."

"Can a raptor see us if we're not moving?" Ada says. "Maybe we can freeze and become invisible."

"Except it's not a real dinosaur," I say, earning myself an angry *"shush"* from Ada.

"Actually," Rube says, making me jump. I didn't know he was back. "Dinosaurs probably had vision similar to modern-day birds of prey."

Emily winces. "So we run. Got it. Shall we go then?"

"Wait, now?" I say.

She shrugs. "We're as prepared as we'll ever be."

"We're not in any way prepared!" I say, but they're already walking towards the shortcut into the kitchen zone.

"Hurry up, Olive," Jack says. "A predator will pick you off if you don't stick with the herd."

I quickly pick up a cola bottle sweet that Ada's dropped, then follow them through the narrow passageway. It's not like I have much choice. We peer out into the half-lit kitchen sets. There's no sign of the dinosaur.

"Let's hunt," Ada says.

"Engage stealth mode," Jack says, swishing his cloak.

The plug trailing from Emily's table lamp clatters against the floor and keeps catching on corners. We weave through the sets until we reach the shiny chrome kitchen. There's nothing here. The only sign of our dramatic escape is the utensils scattered across the floor. I pick them up and hang them back on their hooks.

"How do we get it to show itself?" Ada says, sounding disappointed.

"What were we doing last time it appeared?" Rube says.

Emily screws up her face as she thinks. "Um, Olive was shouting at us for pranking her, only we weren't."

"Shout at us again," Jack says. "Maybe there's something about the high-pitched whine of your voice that attracts dinosaurs."

"What?" I gasp.

"I don't mean that in a horrid way," he says quickly. "Just ... like a dog whistle."

"Maybe they're attracted to fear," Rube says mysteriously.

"Boo!" Jack says, jumping at me with his arms waving around.

"Stop it," I snap. "What's wrong with you?"

"Mostly, I'm hungry," Jack sighs. "I suppose I'm also—"

"It wasn't a question that needed an answer!" I stomp off towards the aisles of kitchen products. "Leave me alone."

I know I shouldn't separate myself from the group. Like Jack said, a predator could pick me off. Only I'm getting far too annoyed with everyone, and I don't want to lose my temper and shout at them. I need some peace and quiet for a few minutes.

Obviously, this doesn't happen. Because the moment I lose sight of the others, I get this shiver up my spine that tells me I am no longer alone.

HUNTED

Shops are always creepy at night. Like when you look through the windows of the supermarket after it's closed, and the empty aisles look *wrong*. Somewhere that's usually heaving with people shouldn't be so empty and silent. Flatpack has that same feeling of emptiness, but it's not silent.

There's a quiet scratching sound coming from nearby. I creep along an aisle of kitchen accessories, turning as I do so nothing can jump out at me. Shelves loom overhead, making me feel tiny and very alone. I'm surrounded by mixing bowls, cutlery, utensils, cake tins, saucepans, oven gloves, pepper grinders. So much stuff, and none of it's any use in my current predicament. I pick up a whisk and hold it out in front of me like a sword. It will have to do.

I edge past a whole display of kitchen taps. They cast weird shadows that remind me of reaching fingers. With my heart in my mouth, I peek around a corner, expecting to see a dinosaur shadow. But there's nothing there. I almost start to relax. But a prickle on the back of my neck warns me there's something behind me.

I turn slowly. There's a hunched shadow on the wall next to a shelf of pet supplies – bowls and beds, that sort of thing. The shadow is almost a dog, only not quite. I reckon it's the size of a small horse but much more muscular. Bear-like. There are two horns sticking out of the sides of its head.

I take a step backwards, and another. It hasn't seen me. A few more steps and I can run to the opposite side of the zone, where I hope I'll be safe. Just a few more—

A loud squeak makes both me and the shadow freeze. I've stepped on a chew toy that's been left on the floor. It's a cute little ghost with a smiley face.

The shadow lifts its head towards me. "N ... nice doggy," I babble.

I see the shadows of its teeth silhouetted on the wall. Drool dangles from its lip. No, that's too much. I throw my whisk at its head and I run. I don't think I've ever run so fast in my life.

I bump into baskets and skid on the concrete. My elbow knocks into a shelf and a whole stack of plates slides to the floor. They smash into a thousand pieces that will take forever to clean up.

I dodge the flying pieces of china and keep running. But I lose my footing on the Pink Brick Road's garish paint. I slide and crash into a display of tiling options. Quickly, I crawl underneath and hold my breath, not wanting to give my position away. Claws scratch at the floor as the creature approaches. Maybe if I'm quiet, it won't find me. All I have to do is stay absolutely, completely silent.

"Olive?" Jack's incredibly loud voice calls. "Where are you, Olive?"

"Come out already," Ada shouts. "Stop hiding."

So much for silence.

Their stomping feet round the corner and Rube spots me. "She's here," he yells. "Everyone, over here!"

"*Shush*," I whisper, trying to wave them away. But it's too late. The shadow rises on a wall of porcelain sinks. It's massive, even bigger than before.

"Poo on a stick!" Jack says, staggering backwards. "What is that?"

"I think it's a bear," Emily whispers.

I shake my head. It's not a bear, it's a demonic hellhound. Which is much, much worse. The shadow whips a long tongue over its teeth. It crouches, like it's going to attack.

"Positions, everyone," Ada says, lifting her phone. "Like we practised."

"Really?" Rube says.

"This is what we're here for." Ada clicks her fingers at Jack. "You're up. Come on."

Jack hurls a handful of meatpops at the hellhound. Nothing happens. Emily swings her light. It makes a loud clunk against the porcelain sinks. The shadow vanishes and immediately reappears on another wall.

"Um," Rube says, "I don't think this plan is going to work."

"We may have underestimated our opponent," Ada admits, backing away slowly.

"What do we do?" Emily says.

"Run!" Jack shouts. He charges off towards the houseplant zone without a backward look. His arms wave in the air like they're windsocks.

I climb out from under the display and we run after Jack into the houseplant zone. Only there's something blocking our path. Somehow, the hellhound has got ahead of us and is waiting at the main entrance on to the showroom floor.

"How did it get here so fast?" Emily says.

"Quick, before it sees us." Ada ducks behind a display of spider plants. We're right next to the path that leads to the unfinished Flatpack museum. Jack, Emily and I came through here earlier.

We all crouch down with the leaves tickling our faces. Through the legs of the table, I see a shadow slip around the corner. The truth hits me – that hellhound at the entrance didn't get ahead of us. There's two of them, stalking us through the foliage.

"Why's it not a raptor?" Jack whispers. "I miss the dinosaur."

"Does it make any difference *what* eats us?" Emily says. "Eaten is eaten."

"I don't think it would be fun to be eaten by a crocodile," Rube says.

I shudder. Crocodiles terrify me. They have ever since Papa showed me some old *Peter Pan* film. He thought it would be less traumatic for me than the scary films Dad likes to watch. It was not less traumatic.

"Or ants," Rube adds. "Millions of ants would be the worst. Did you know bullet ants have the worst sting of any insect, although I don't think they'd eat you."

"Can we not?" I say, adding a new horror to the catalogue of things that terrify me.

"I can't get a good angle," Ada complains. She's trying to film the hellhound shadow but the plants are getting in the way, plus the phone's camera won't focus.

"Is that what matters right now?" I say.

"It's all that matters," she says.

"Um, actually," Rube whispers, "I think *that's* what matters right now." He points to where Karen and the twins have appeared at the entrance to the showroom. We all fumble with our torches, turning them off before the adults spot us.

Karen strides into the zone, not noticing the

hellhound shadow at the entrance. The massive, drooling hellhound that looks like it could swallow us all in one gulp! Only, I guess it's not in the mood for dinner right now as it takes one look at Karen and vanishes from sight.

"That's handy," Emily whispers.

"That's very annoying," Ada complains.

I shush them all. We duck lower as Karen approaches our position. A pager on Rube's belt buzzes loudly. Karen and the twins have activated one of the sensors Rube placed earlier. He quickly silences it and mouths *"sorry"*.

Karen narrows her eyes and squints through the darkness in our direction. "I know there's someone in here," she says.

"We already searched the place," one of the twins says.

"There's no sign of any kids," his brother adds.

Karen bends down and picks up something from the floor. From a distance, it looks like a poo. She sniffs it, then gives it a small lick.

"Noooo," one of the twins says, recoiling.

"It's a meatpop, you fool," she snaps, throwing it at him. "Someone's in here. Find them. Now!"

We all hold our breath as Karen and the twins march right towards us. There's no way they're not going to spot us. It's only a matter of time.

Only then, one of the twins cries out in his high-pitched voice. "I saw something! Behind that shelf."

They all move in the opposite direction. My relief is short-lived. One of the hellhound shadows peels itself out of a dark corner and moves towards us. A second appears. I knew there were two! It cuts off our way out of the showroom. It's almost like they were waiting for the three adults to get out of the way.

"We need to run," I whisper.

"We can't while Karen is so close," Emily says. "She'll see us."

"The shadows!" I hiss.

The first hellhound gets closer and closer. Silhouetted on the walls, I can see its muscles rippling and the drool that drops from its open mouth. I press myself against the wall and try to will Karen to hurry up and leave.

The shadow gets closer. There are weird spikes all over its body.

"Rats," Karen says. "It's definitely rats."

"Ew, gross," one of the twins says.

"All right, new plan," Karen barks. "You two, search the showroom *properly*. I'll deal with the furry vermin. Let's go."

Finally, they're leaving. We all wait for their footsteps to fade away. Then we run for the door leading to the Flatpack museum. It's the only place we can go.

I think we're going to make it, but then Jack screams. "Something's got me!"

I can't see much because none of us have our torches on, but I think Jack's cape has snagged on something. He jerks backwards like he's been given a sharp tug.

"Help me!" he says, clinging on to the edges of a shelving unit.

Emily, Rube and Ada all grab him and hold on to his arms. They're not strong enough. Their fingers slip and he is pulled down on to his belly. I think there's something tangled up in his cape. Whatever it is, it's not a gigantic hellhound – it's far too small. So how is it dragging Jack backwards across the floor?

"The cape!" I say. "Undo the cape."

Jack unties the bow around his neck and fights his way out of the curtain. It's whipped away into a narrow space between some shelves. Emily and Ada help Jack to his feet and we all throw ourselves through the door into the museum. The five of us lean our weight back against the door to close it.

We're only just in time. Something heavy slams into the opposite side, once, twice, three times. I think it's going to burst through the wood, but the door holds. The slamming stops and everything goes quiet except for our panting breaths.

"You know, capes are pretty dangerous," Jack says, rubbing his neck where the string was pulled tight. "Someone should have thought about that sooner."

WOOD FOR THE TREES

We keep leaning against the door until we're sure nothing's about to come bursting through. Tentatively, we step away. Whatever it was that grabbed Jack, it's gone. We're safe. For now, at least.

"That was intense," Jack says. "Please say you got that on film, Ada."

Ada's looking at the footage on her phone and frowning. "Nothing's in focus," she says angrily. "The camera is rubbish. It's like it can't even *see* the shadows."

"The shadows don't make sense," I say quietly, still thinking about how we've only seen shadows of dinosaurs and hellhounds, never the monsters themselves. "They don't *match*."

"What do you mean?" Emily asks.

"The thing that got hold of Jack was small, but the shadows are huge. They don't match."

Rube nods slowly. "Lots of animals display what's called 'deimatic behaviour' in the wild. It's—"

"You lost me at 'lots'," Jack says.

"Shock and awe," Rube says. "Some animals will try to scare away a predator by making themselves look bigger and fiercer. An example is a bird called the bittern. When startled, it hisses and spreads its wings to reveal huge fake eyes that make it look like a monster."

I think Rube's on to something. I shine my torch at the wall and use my hand to make a shadow-puppet crocodile. When I move the torch away, the crocodile grows and grows. It's much scarier than the hand casting it.

"So the dinosaur and dog shadows aren't real?" Emily says. "The real monsters are making their shadows big and scary so we'll be scared of them? Like a defence mechanism?"

"Except those things aren't defenceless," Jack says, pulling a face. "One of them tried to drag me off, remember?"

"Maybe they use the shadows as a way to herd their prey," I say. "Like a pack of lions hunting wildebeest."

"I'm with Olive," Emily says. "They definitely wanted to eat us."

Ada sighs dramatically. "None of this helps solve the problem at hand."

"The not-being-eaten problem?" I say meekly.

"The having-no-proof-that-the-monsters-are-real problem!" She strides down the corridor, her hair bobbing angrily. "Where are we anyway? Someone tell me where we are!"

"A museum," I say, going after her. "The Flatpack Experience. Emily, Jack and I saw it earlier."

The corridor is decorated with blueprints of Flatpack's most famous products. I notice they all have QR codes beneath them, meaning you can buy copies to go on your own walls. Dad would love the pineapple.

"Weirdness alert, weirdness alert," Jack says, shining his torch around a corner. "What the custard cream is *that*?"

He's found what looks like a fairytale entrance to a forest. A moulded archway is painted to look like a pair of trees, bent over with their branches entwined. The archway leads through into a dark room. Everyone else walks straight in, because of course they do.

A light comes on automatically, so we switch off our torches. It's the strangest room I've ever been in. The whole place is decorated to look like a literal forest, only it's made of painted fibreglass. It reminds me of the Santa's grotto at the garden centre, only without all the artificial snow and robot polar bears.

Fake trees grow out of a brown, leafy carpet. There are grassy hillocks and plastic ferns. The ceiling is completely covered with leaves and branches to make it look like a woodland canopy. The walls are painted with more trees, the forest stretching away from us in every direction. It's peaceful after the in-your-face "buy me, buy me, buy me" of the showroom. I can't see a single QR code or basket of products for sale. There's also a notable absence of Flatpack furniture.

There are information boards fixed to some of the trees and walls. They tell the Flatpack story but, quite frankly, I'm not interested. I sit against a tree trunk and clunk my head back against the hollow plastic. Rube sits next to me and offers me half a vegan cheese sandwich.

My tummy gurgles, so I accept. I take the tiniest bite and try to chew, but it doesn't want to go down.

"Ada misses you," Rube says out of nowhere.

My stomach clenches. I don't know what I'm supposed to say. I force myself to swallow the bite of sandwich and it's like swallowing a rock.

"I highly doubt that," I choke out.

If Ada wanted to be friends with me, she wouldn't have ditched me so easily after our falling out in class. She would have fought to keep me instead of moving straight on to Rube. But then a little voice in my head reminds me I didn't fight for her either.

"I mean, she hasn't said anything. But I can tell," Rube clarifies.

"I don't think we were very good for each other," I say. "I don't hate her or anything. We just grew apart."

"Maybe you could grow back together," he says hopefully.

"Why's it matter to you?" I say, more grumpily than I mean to.

"Because I want you both to be happy," he says.

I take another bite of the sandwich so I don't have

to say anything else. I watch Emily and Jack across the room. They're trying to swing from branch to branch through the trees, laughing when Jack repeatedly falls down. I can't imagine being that relaxed and happy around anyone. Not Ada, not Emily, not even myself.

"Ipsley Island," Ada shouts through a mouthful of sweets. "Where have I heard that name before?"

"Is it where they filmed that TV series?" Jack says. "The one where the prize was a day out with a prince?"

"No, that was in the Caribbean," Emily says. "I've never heard of Ipsley Island."

"Me neither," I say.

Ada paces, chewing on her fingernail. "I'm sure I've heard of it before."

"What's the significance?" Rube says.

Ada gestures to one of the information boards. "Ipsley Island is where Flatpack source 87% of their wood. It's off the coast of Scotland."

"So what?" Emily says.

"There's something about the name that seems familiar, but I can't work out what it is."

Ada goes back to looking around the museum.

Emily and Jack go back to messing around in the trees. They all seem so calm. It's like they've already forgotten we were chased in here by a pair of hellhounds, right after nearly being eaten by a dinosaur.

My stomach lurches and I set the sandwich aside. I get to my feet because I need to take my mind off all the worrying. Rube scurries behind me. "It's weird to have a museum in a furniture store, don't you think?" he says.

"Yeah, I guess," I mumble, not wanting to get into a conversation about it.

"I suppose Flatpack has become part of our cultural heritage in recent years," he muses. "A way of life and not just a shop."

"My dads would agree with you on that."

"You know, for a long time, it was thought that humans were the only species to pass cultural knowledge down the generations. But some think pigeons can do it too. Pigeons are interesting animals."

Rube continues to talk about pigeons as we circle the room, looking at all the information boards. They detail the entire history of Flatpack, from its origins as a small chain selling pine furniture, to the giant it is today. Ipsley

Island seems to have played a big role in its success.

According to the museum, Ipsley is one of the largest uninhabited islands in the British Isles. In the photos, it's all mountains, forests and rugged coastlines. It's a twenty-minute boat ride from the mainland – the Flatpack workers make the trip there and back every day.

"Pigeons are also one of the only animals to pass the mirror test," Rube continues.

"Why do you think no one lives on Ipsley?" I gesture at the photos of the island.

Rube cocks his head and reads the information board I'm looking at. He takes out his phone and searches for something. "Aha, this is interesting. Ipsley wasn't always uninhabited. It was once home to a small settlement of humans. However, it was abandoned well over a hundred years ago and people have never returned."

"The big question is, why was it abandoned?" I say.

THE MYSTERY OF IPSLEY ISLAND

We all stand around the poster board and stare at the photos of Ipsley Island. I try to stop imagining what it would be like to be trapped alone on an isolated island, so far away from anyone else. No, scrap that. Not trapped alone. Trapped with *something* else.

"Maybe everyone left because there weren't enough people to make a football team," Emily says.

"Yes, I'm sure it was that," Ada says sarcastically.

"I wouldn't want to live there," Jack says. "I bet the Wi-Fi is terrible."

"OK, this video is interesting," Rube says, tapping at his phone. "Take a look."

We gather around him and peer at the phone over his shoulder. He's paused a video titled: *Cryptic Cryptids – Strange Shadows on Ipsley Island.*

"Cryptic Cryptids!" Ada says. "He's one of the top cryptozoologists around. I've seen all his videos."

Rube shakes his head. "Maybe not all of them. He made this video about Ipsley Island a few years ago but almost immediately took it back down. Luckily someone made a copy in time and shared it on a cryptids forum."

"Once something is on the internet, it's there forever," Jack says seriously.

"Why did he take it down?" Emily says.

"It wouldn't be the first time Flatpack has suppressed information," Ada says. "Look at what they're doing with the Hashtag Haunted Flatpack situation."

"I'm going to play it," Rube says.

In the video, a person wearing a scary bald dog mask sits in a dim room, lit only by candles. "Welcome to Cryptic Cryptids," he says, except what comes out is more like "Cricket cryptics". He tries again. "Cryptid Crypigs." Then he gives up.

"Today, I want to tell you the story of Ipsley Island," he says.

He talks about Ipsley, repeating a lot of the same information I've already read on the museum's displays. Then he gets on to the abandoned settlement and his image is replaced by drone photographs of an old village surrounded by trees.

"The question is," the dog man says, leaning close to the camera, "why did the people leave in the first place?"

"Because it's cold and rainy?" Emily says.

"Let me tell you the story of the campers," he says. "Ipsley stood untouched for close to a hundred years after it was abandoned. That was until forty years ago, when a small group of hikers hired a private boat and went there for a week-long camping expedition."

The image changes to one of a couple of tattered tents, billowing in a small clearing in the middle of a wooded area.

"The campers happened upon the remains of an old settlement. In one house, there were cups and plates still on the tables, doors swinging open, the remains of clothes on the washing lines. It appeared that the original inhabitants had upped and left without even packing their belongings."

"What happened to the campers?" Jack says, jiggling up and down. "Oh no, it was something horrible, wasn't it?"

"The first night on the island," the dog man says, "the hikers pitched their tents within dense woodland and settled down to sleep. They were awoken by strange noises. Snapping twigs. Scuttling sounds. Scratches at the fabric of their tent. And then there were the shadows."

"Shadows?" I cross my arms to stop my hands from shaking.

"Shadows that it simply wasn't possible to explain. Terrifying shadows dragged straight from their worst nightmares. Creatures with claws and gaping mouths. Monsters!"

I jump at his sudden exclamation.

"They immediately packed up their belongings, leaving their tents pitched where they stood. Even though it was the middle of the night, they boarded their boat to the mainland and vowed never to return."

Rube stops the video and lowers the phone. "It sounds like the same shadow monsters the campers saw are now here, living in Flatpack."

"They must have hitched a ride with the wood used to make the Flatpack furniture," Ada says.

There's a long pause while we all take it in. I think about what the Cryptic Cryptids man said: "Terrifying shadows dragged straight from their worst nightmares." It's true. The shadows I've seen are *my* worst nightmares. Spiders, hellhounds, dinosaurs. It's almost as if the creatures know what I'm scared of and they're using it against me.

I raise my hand. "Um, you know how the entire village fled the island because of these creatures?" I say. "And then the hikers left in the night because they were so scared?"

"Yeah, what of it?" Jack says.

"Do you think *maybe* it's a sign we should *maybe* all go home too?"

Ada looks at me like I've sprouted a second head. "Why on Earth would we want to do that?" she says.

"Olive does have a good point," Emily says. "We

went looking for the monsters and it was a disaster."

"Because we didn't know what we were dealing with," Ada says.

"Er, we still don't know what we're dealing with?" Jack says.

"Which is why we need to gather data!"

"No," I say. "I'm not doing it."

"Then stay here," Ada snaps. "By yourself, all alone. If you're too—"

"*Shush!*" Emily says.

I think she's jumping to my defence, but the reality is she's heard something. A door creaks open at the end of the corridor. Muffled voices reach us. Our eyes widen. We all duck behind the trees. The lights are all on, though. It won't take much for Karen to see us.

"I keep finding cola bottle sweets on the floor," Karen says. "The kids must be in the store."

"How are we supposed to find them without the CCTV?" one of the twins says.

"Do we even need to find them?" the other man says. "I mean, if we leave them alone maybe they'll leave us alone. A bit like the rats."

"Listen here," Karen snarls, "I am not letting a bunch of snot-nosed kids get the better of me. We are going to find them, and when we do…" She claps her hands together, making me jump.

"We could call the police?" one of the twins says.

"The police?" she says quietly. "The police?"

"It was just an idea. No need to stare at me like that, it's scary."

"If we call the police, how are we going to explain why *we're* here, hmm?" Karen says through gritted teeth.

"Oh. Yeah, you're right, boss."

"You really do have meatpops for brains," she snaps. "Get the torches and Mr Sticky. We're going hunting." She strides past the museum with the twins at her heels.

I think we've got away with it. Then Jack opens his mouth. "Mr Sticky?" he says. "Ohh, he sounds fun!"

"Shhhh," Emily hisses, but it's too late.

"Children," Karen says, her footsteps halting. "I hear children."

ON THE RUN, AGAIN

"Run!" Ada shouts.

Tripping over roots and clambering over hillocks, we weave through the trees. We race out of the museum and nearly collide with Karen, the twins and Mr Sticky who, perhaps unsurprisingly, is a massive extendable pole. The sort you'd use to open high-up windows or swat down hard-to-reach cobwebs.

One of the twins tries to use Mr Sticky to block our path. We all duck underneath, except for Jack who unintentionally limbos. We bounce off the walls as we run. Karen and the twins are a few metres behind us.

"Stop them!" Karen screams. "Hurry up, you fools."

Mr Sticky is getting in their way. He's too long to comfortably fit and keeps snagging on the light fittings. By the time we push open the doors back to the houseplant zone, we have a bit of a lead on the store workers. Fighting our way through the foliage, we head for the exit from the showroom. But then the twin wielding Mr Sticky takes a different route and he gets there first. He thwacks the pole across our path. Screaming, we run in the opposite direction. We skid around one of the pot plant displays and come face to face with the second twin.

"Got you now," he says, making a grab for Emily.

She does a knee slide under his outstretched arms and across the floor. When he tries to grab her again, she rolls under a display and out the other side. He tries to follow and smacks his head against the table. A plastic cactus topples over and lands on him.

We run for the secret passageway through to the kitchen zone. I'm panicking so much I barely have time to worry about the shadow monsters, and where they might be. We dart through the kitchen sets, but Karen and the twins continue to chase us.

It's not like when the raptor stalked us through these same kitchens. Karen and the twins don't stick to the dark, shadowy places. They barrel through the zone, knocking things over and shining megawatt torches at us. We can't hide until we put some distance between us and them. Our only choice is to keep running.

Emily sweeps a basket of plastic lemons and limes off a table. They get beneath the adults' feet, buying us a few extra seconds. We skid around a corner into the bathroom zone. It's instantly darker than everywhere we've been so far. Maybe we can lose them in here.

Around the edge of the zone, there are long aisles showcasing all the different basin options, toilet lids, shower curtains, taps and everything else you could possibly need in a bathroom. In the centre of the space, there are several interconnected bathroom sets. Combined, the sets are the size of an entire bungalow. I think about hiding inside, but there are only two ways in and out. We'd be trapped.

"Down here," Ada says.

We run along one of the aisles and hide at the far end, behind a display of floor tiles. I peek out around the corner. A few moments later, Karen and the twins appear in the zone. I'm hoping they'll go straight past, but this time they don't.

"Do you hear footsteps?" Karen says.

"I can't hear anything but a ringing noise in my ears," one of the twins says, holding his head. There's a large bump on his temple.

"They're hiding somewhere in here," Karen says. "You. Bob. Watch the exits from the zone. Bill can help me search the sets."

Bob – the twin with the head injury – goes to stand guard. He positions himself on top of a toilet so he has a view of both the entrance and exit to the zone. There are no secret passageways according to Ada's map. No other ways out.

Karen, Bill and Mr Sticky disappear inside the bathroom sets at the centre of the zone. I hear a shower curtain being torn aside. Cupboards and loo seats slam. Karen's torch shines out of the little windows in the rooms, briefly lighting up slashes of the zone.

"What are we going to do?" Rube whispers.

"We could rush Bob over there?" Emily says,

gesturing to the twin watching the exits to the zone. He's half-crouched with his arms extended, like he's preparing for a wrestling match.

"I think he's ready for us this time," Ada says.

I try to work out if there's a way to escape. I don't think trying to fight is an option. There are three of them, plus Mr Sticky. I don't think we can win, even if we do arm ourselves with loo brushes and bath toys. Running and hiding is our only choice.

"We need a distraction," I say. "Maybe we can make them think we've run through into bedrooms. Then they'll be in there forever, searching under every bed and in all the wardrobes. But instead of going that way, we can escape into kitchens."

"That's a good plan," Rube says.

"Big brain," Jack says, trying to high-five me.

Ada swats his hand aside. "It's the best plan we have, I suppose. But it doesn't cover how we're going to distract him."

"We could streak through the zone!" Jack says.

"No," we all reply.

"I'm a good thrower," Emily says.

"Well done," Ada snaps, rolling her eyes. "I don't see how that's relevant."

Emily takes down a net bag full of small plastic sea creatures from a shelf. "I can throw these into bedrooms and it will make them think that's where we are."

It might work. But we need to hurry. Karen and Bill won't be searching the sets for much longer. We tiptoe to the next aisle and Emily rips open the bag of toys. She carefully selects a killer whale. Then she does some light stretches.

"When you're ready," Ada complains.

Emily shoots her a dirty look, then throws the whale as hard as she can. It whizzes through the archway leading into the bedroom zone, where it collides with a wardrobe, making a dull thud. It bounces across the floor in what sounds a lot like running footsteps.

"Over there! I saw something!" Bob shouts. He runs from his post and into bedrooms, as we planned.

Karen and Bill burst out of the bathroom sets and go after him. "How did they get past you?" she snaps. "You had one job!"

"I was watching, honest. They must have teleported."

We wait until the adults are out of sight, then we go. We're going to have to run across the Pink Brick Road, which means we'll be out in the open. Emily and Jack go first, Rube scurrying behind them with his bag weighing him down. Once they've ducked behind a wall of toilet seats, Ada and I check the coast is still clear and begin to cross. Except a noise makes us hesitate and we both look around, trying to identify its source.

It's a quiet scuttling noise, like claws on concrete.

"Come on," Emily hisses from her hiding place, waving at us.

We don't move, though. Emily can't see it, but we can. On the wall between us and the other three, there's a shadow. A giant spider, exactly like the one we saw in my attic spare room, all those months ago.

ADMIT YOU LIED

The spider quivers, readying itself to attack. Then it lunges. The shadow melts between walls, closer and closer. As it passes across the shelves of bathroom tiles and rows of toilets and sinks, its shape distorts. Its long legs bend at terrible angles. Its body wobbles like a big water balloon.

Ada stares at it in awe. "Amazing," she whispers.

"Move!" I say, yanking her into the bathroom sets. It's the only place I can think of where we can hide. We press ourselves back against the wall. I can't breathe. My heart has become an old kitchen sponge, dried up at the back of the cupboard.

"I knew it was real," Ada says. "I was right, and you were wrong."

"Are you serious?" I whisper. "Is now the time?"

"I'd like to hear you admit you lied about not seeing the spider to impress Emily."

"What?" I widen my eyes and shake my head. "We're being chased by a furious shop manager and shadow monsters that intend to eat us. But you want to argue about who is right?"

"It's not an *argument*, Olive. Like you said, there's a shadow monster right there. Clearly, I'm the one who was right."

One of the spider shadow's legs reaches around the edge of the door. I scream and take off at a run through the dark bathroom sets, with Ada behind me. The security lights aren't doing much to brighten the rooms. It's like when you get up in the night for a wee and have to feel your way to the toilet. Except Ada and I don't know where everything is, so we keep running into things.

Something scuttles and I know the monster is now in here with us. I can smell the woods. I'm starting to realize that anywhere they've been smells like mud and rotting leaves. That's why so much Flatpack furniture ends up being stored in the mysterious Warehouse Two. Because the monsters make it stink.

Another burst of scuttling makes me jump. A plastic plant tickles me, and I immediately imagine a spider trying to climb inside my clothes. I scream and do a little dance, slapping at my T-shirt.

"Stop screaming," Ada says. "You're going to give us away to Karen and her sidekicks."

I think it's a bit late for that. Besides, I'd happily be captured by Karen if it means I can escape that awful spider. I can hear it scurrying across the bathroom tiles in the room behind us. I don't want to look and see how close it is.

"In here," Ada says, climbing into a big porcelain bath with silver paws for feet.

It sits in the middle of the room with a circular shower curtain half-drawn around it. We pull the curtain closed and sit down in the bath. We automatically huddle together, even though I don't think either of us wants to be this close. Something scratches at the underside of the bath. I shuffle even closer to Ada.

"Don't worry, it's not real," she whispers. "Only little kids believe in monsters."

"This isn't the time for sarcasm," I hiss. "There's something out there."

"I'm sure Emily, your best friend, will be here to help you soon." She pretends to look for Emily. "Oh, no, she ran off and left you here."

"Why are you being so mean?"

"*I'm* mean? Ha! Good one."

A shadow rises outside the shower curtain and our argument is cut short. The curtain is a flimsy white thing, so I can see every little hair on the spider's long knobbly legs. I can even see the bulges of its eyes and the way it quivers. It's putting on an up-close and personal shadow puppet show for us.

Ada slides lower in the bath and pulls her unicorn hood over her head. She holds a finger over her lips. The spider shadow looks like it's sniffing the air, trying to find us. Maybe if we're quiet, it will pass us by. I stay as still as possible. Finally, the shadow grows blurry

and shrinks in size.
I think it's moved
away from the bath
to search the rest of
the room.

"Uh-oh," Ada
whispers.

She points. There's
a real spider climbing
up the curtain. A literal
house spider, the size
of a fifty pence coin,
with hairy legs and wiggly
feelers. My eyes widen and
I press myself back against
the side of the bath.

The spider clambers
on to the curtain
rail. Like a circus
performer, it steps
over the curtain
rings. Only it scurries

too fast and gets into a wobble. I think it's going to fall. I suck in a breath to scream, but Ada clamps her hand over my mouth.

We both watch as the spider rights itself. It follows the circular shower rail and climbs on to the shower head. It's right above me now. Chilling out directly over my head. One wrong step and all my nightmares will come true.

A scuttling sound reminds me that a house spider isn't our biggest problem right now. The giant spider shadow circles the bath. It pauses. Comes closer. Feet scrabble against the porcelain, reminding me of my dog when he wants to get through a closed door. We still don't know what the monsters actually look like. Something with a lot of claws.

As if that wasn't bad enough, the house spider above me gets too close to the edge of the shower head. It slips and ends up dangling by two legs. It struggles as it tries to pull itself back up. I shuffle myself up against the plug end, as far away from it as possible.

Ada shakes her head at me, warning me not to scream. I grit my teeth, but I don't think I can hold out much longer. The spider on the shower head is still dangling. I keep imagining it landing on my head and getting tangled in my hair. I genuinely think I would die of fear if that happened.

The shower curtain shakes. Whatever's out there is trying to get in. It yanks hard enough that it rattles the curtain rail. The real-life house spider is somehow still clinging on. But if the shadow monster keeps shaking the curtain rail, the vibrations will loosen the spider and it will fall.

"What do we do?" I whisper.

"You're the one with all the plans," Ada says, her eyes not leaving the house spider. She isn't easily scared, but I don't suppose anyone wants something with eight legs landing on them.

A torch beam shines into the bathroom through a little window. "I think they're in here," Karen's voice says. "Where's Mr Sticky?"

"Oh no," Ada murmurs.

It's not all bad, though. Because as footsteps race through the bathroom sets, the giant spider shadow shrinks away and the house spider manages to climb back on to the shower head. I can breathe again, for a second at least.

Then Karen starts to whack at the shower curtain with Mr Sticky. "Get out of the bath, now!" she bellows. "Out! Now!"

The curtain whips against my bare arms and face. And then it happens. Karen hits the curtain so hard it rips away from the rail. The house spider chooses this moment to abandon ship and it makes a leap from the shower head.

My body goes into autopilot. Without even thinking, I try to throw myself out of the bath. Ada does the same. Our sudden shift in weight is too much for the badly manufactured tub, and it tips.

Ada and I tumble out on to the floor, and find ourselves face to face with *the* most hideous creature I have ever seen.

THE WORLD'S SMALLEST OFFICE

A pale, wrinkled *thing* flies towards my face. It's the size of a guinea pig but completely hairless. Its face has tiny black eyes and a red snout. It has two long front legs with huge claws, but no back legs at all. Instead, it has a long moist tail, like a slug's.

The *thing* stretches out its long front legs like it's planning to scratch out my eyes. Its mouth opens in a horrible squeal and I see all its yellow teeth sticking out at funny angles. I scream and it screams, and Karen screams because the shower curtain has wrapped itself around her face making her look like a rubbish Halloween ghost.

Everyone is screaming, apart from Ada. She's trying to record the *thing* on her phone.

At the last second, it decides it's not going to eat my face. It breaks off the attack and scuttles behind the toilet. It leaves behind a long trail of slime. Slime that smells like the forest.

"Bother," Ada says, lowering her phone. "I wasn't quick enough."

"Get this off me," Karen shouts, still struggling beneath the shower curtain.

"I've got you, boss," one of the twins says.

He tries to help her, but it's not a very big set, and five people is too many. Karen accidentally hits him in the face with Mr Sticky and he yelps in pain.

"Let's go," Ada says, crawling between the man's legs and heading for the door.

I move to crawl after her, but the house spider scuttles out from under Karen's shower curtain and nearly touches my shoe. I sit back heavily on my bum with my knees tucked up. It's too much. I feel like my chest is going to explode and then all my internal organs will fly out of me.

"Olive, come on," Ada says.

I shake my head.

Karen finally manages to tear the curtain off her face. "You," she says, pointing at me. "Do not move."

I couldn't move if I wanted to. All my limbs have betrayed me and they're no longer taking orders from my brain. Ada looks between me and Karen, then, with a brief shrug, she runs away.

"What are you waiting for?" Karen barks. "Go after her!"

The twins trip out of the bathroom sets and I'm alone with Karen. I swallow heavily. Karen's expression is so smug, you'd think she'd just won employee of the century.

"I've got you now," she says, checking her reflection in a mirror. She quickly tries to flatten her messy hair.

Strictly speaking, it wasn't her who got me. It was a house spider and a terrifying rat-slug. But she's obviously going to take all the credit. I find I don't care. This night has gone on for too long and her calling my parents will be a big relief, even when I do get into trouble.

She marches me through the bathroom zone and into kitchens. I glance around, trying to work out where the others have gone. There's no sign of them. I can't hear Ada or the twins either. Everything is quiet, apart from Karen's noisy shoes clicking on the Pink Brick Road.

Passing through dining rooms, we reach the sofa zone. She takes me through a staff-only door. It's the door Rube placed a sensor on earlier. It leads to a staircase and a goods lift that must go down to the main warehouse. It's presumably the lift where Karen and the twins took that stolen sofa.

"In you go," Karen says, still sounding pleased with herself as she gestures to the lift.

Head down, I shuffle into the dingy metal box. It smells funny, and there are torn labels stuck to the floor and walls. There's a mirror on one side, in which Karen once again tries to fix her hair. She fluffs up the bits on the top and then licks her fingers to smooth the fringe. Noticing my repulsed expression, she stops.

The lift clunks to a halt. "OK, move," she tells me.

We step out into the warehouse. It is even bigger than the showroom. Without all the little sets, its vastness feels intimidating. The metal shelves go all the way up to the ceiling, as high as a two-storey house. The aisles seem to be endlessly long, and they're all deserted.

There are pink arrows and road markings on the concrete floor. The walls are corrugated metal. There's a long window that looks through to the public collection area. That's where people pick up the warehouse products they've selected using the Flatpack app.

I can make out the tills beyond the collection area, and the closed-up meatpop stand right by the exit doors. I'm hoping Karen will take me in that direction. Maybe she's going to throw me out into the night. I'd prefer the cold and the dark to staying inside this store for a minute longer. But she goes in the opposite direction, leading us to the very far end of the warehouse.

"Where are we going?" I whisper.

"My office," she snaps. "Hurry up."

It's not what I would call an office. The whole thing isn't much bigger than my bathroom at home. There are two chairs and an old-fashioned set of metal drawers. On one wall, there's a corkboard on which she's pinned dozens of newspaper articles. When she slams the door, they ripple like feathers on a bird.

We do an awkward little dance as she attempts to squeeze past me to get to her own chair. It's such a tight fit in here. I'm not sure it's even meant to be an office. More like she's repurposed a forgotten cupboard for her own use. The room smells like onions and sausages.

"Can we call my parents?" I ask.

She ignores me and roots around in the top drawer. She brings out a Tupperware box containing about twenty closely packed sausage rolls. She pops a sausage roll into her mouth whole and stares at me as she chews. Her smug expression still hasn't faded.

"I knew you kids were still in here," she eventually says. "I knew it."

I can smell her meaty breath and it's turning my stomach.

"I want to go home," I say. "Can I call my dad?"

Karen continues to avoid the question. She brushes pastry crumbs off her uniform. "This is *my* store, young lady."

This catches me off guard. "Really? You own Flatpack?"

"What?" She screws up her face. "No, of course I don't own it."

"Oh. Right. I guess that makes sense given that your office is so" – I cringe at the look on her face, but I can't make myself stop speaking – "small."

"You see that?" she says, gesturing to the wall of newspaper clippings. "I have collected every newspaper article mentioning Flatpack for the past ten years. That's how dedicated I am to this store. I am always watching. I know *everything* that happens here."

I gulp heavily, my throat dry. I'm beginning to think Karen's not going to help me.

"What I want to know is what you know," she says.

"What I know?" I ask.

"Why you're here."

"It was a mistake. We got locked in," I say.

"That's the story you're going with?" She helps herself to another sausage roll. "You know what I think? I think you're investigating. A real Nancy Drew, is that right? You came here hoping to bust our operation open?"

I shake my head. I want to reassure her I'm uninterested in her stolen stock. Tell her that I won't tell anyone. Only then she'd know that I know she's stealing from Flatpack. Something tells me this would be a dangerous thing to admit.

"Have you been watching us? Recording our activities, perhaps?"

"No! We didn't see anything."

That last sentence was a mistake.

"You didn't *see* anything? Do you think there's something to see?"

I shake my head.

"Listen here," she says, leaning close to me. "I have put too much into this operation to let a bunch of meddling kids ruin it for me. Tonight is going to set us up for months, and it needs to go off without a hitch. You, little girl, are a hitch."

I can feel a lump in my throat. I don't want to cry. "I don't know anything," I whisper.

"The company AGM happens once a year. It's our one opportunity to take as much stock as possible. Bill and Bob store it in their dad's garage and we sell it through online marketplaces. It's a genius plan. Last year, we made over ten thousand pounds from this operation."

Why is she telling me all of this? The more I know, the more scared I feel. She's going full evil-villain monologue. In films, the monologue always comes right before the villain tries to murder the hero.

"I'm not letting you steal my money from me," she says. "Don't even think about it."

"I don't want your money," I say. "Honest. I just want to go home."

"That," she says, pointing at me with a sausage roll and leaning back in her chair, "is not going to happen."

MARCUS KNIGHT WAS HERE

There's a knock on the door, so I don't get to ask what she means by "that's not going to happen". My mind drifts to thoughts of Marcus Knight, the store worker who clocked in and never clocked out. The Flatpack superstore is not somewhere anyone would choose as their final resting place.

"Isn't this exciting?" Karen says. "I think we've finally caught your little friends."

She sets the sausage rolls on top of the drawers and squeezes past me. I turn my face away, but her bum still bumps me on the way past.

It's the twins at the door. They've got a real sweat on,

like they just stepped out of the gym. "They got away from us," they both say breathlessly.

"For goodness' sake," Karen says. She narrows her eyes at me, then steps outside the office. She closes the door behind her and I hear a key turn.

She's locked me in. Definite villain behaviour.

I check my phone, but there's no reception. There doesn't appear to be a landline in this room either, so calling Dad and Papa is out. I press my ear against the door hoping to hear what's happening outside.

"This is your fault. You were supposed to search the showroom," Karen says. "Those little twerps have been running wild for hours, gathering evidence on us."

"Evidence?" one of the twins squeaks.

"They're trying to expose us," she says. "Or maybe they're planning to extort money from us."

"What does extort mean?"

"Blackmail," the other twin says. "Like, if you don't give me a hundred pounds, we're going to tell everyone you've been stealing from the shop."

"Oh, right. Blackmail. Like Marcus."

"We don't talk about Marcus," his brother says.

"I'm not letting a bunch of kids blackmail me," Karen says. "They know too much. We need to get rid of them."

My blood runs cold. Surely she means throw us out of the shop before we cause any more trouble. Right?

"We need to catch them and make sure they don't go blabbing," Karen continues.

The three of them must move away from the office because I stop being able to hear them. I return to my chair and wait, nervously scuffing my foot against the floor. I don't want to think about what Karen meant when she said "get rid of them", so instead I decide to search the office for a spare key that will get me out of here.

I pull open the top drawer as quietly as possible. It has another box of sausage rolls inside, but nothing else. I'm about to try the next drawer when something on the wall catches my attention. I run my fingers through the curling newspaper articles until they stop on a familiar face. Marcus Knight, with his angry eyes and one gold tooth.

I pull the newspaper article down and skim through

it. The story is remarkably similar to the one Ada told us earlier. Marcus was reported missing by his supervisor after failing to turn up for work for several days, only for his belongings to be discovered in his locker. It was presumed he disappeared to avoid being arrested for a series of burglaries in the area. From the sound of the article, no one was particularly upset that he was gone.

One of the twins mentioned Marcus a minute ago. They said something about blackmail. Add to that burglary and theft? I don't want to sound mean, but at least the shadow monsters chose someone really bad to eat.

I'm suddenly startled by footsteps coming from outside the office. I quickly try to pin the article back up. Except I accidentally unpin a whole stack of clippings. They flutter down to the ground.

"Oh no," I say, trying to gather them up before Karen comes back in and discovers what a mess I've made.

I manage to pin them back up, but bump into the drawers, rattling them noisily. The box of sausage rolls topples off the top. I try to catch it, but I fumble the box and several of the pastries fall out. I squeal in panic.

I toss the dropped sausage rolls back into the box, dusting off the worst of the dirt. A couple have fallen behind the drawers and there are crumbs everywhere. I poke my fingers into the space behind the drawers, trying to flick the lost rolls out of the gap. I retrieve one of them, but it brings something else with it. Something small and smooth is embedded in the pastry. It's a shiny piece of gold. A gold tooth.

How many people have gold teeth these days? Not many that I've seen, so it's not too big a leap to conclude this tooth belonged to none other than Marcus Knight. Which raises the question: why is it not with the rest of him?

I think about how Karen claimed to know everything that happens in this store. I start to wonder if she not only knows about the shadow monsters, but if she's covering up for them. Maybe Karen's aware the creatures dragged poor Marcus off and ate him, leaving only his gold tooth behind. Or maybe, just maybe, she *fed* Marcus to them, knowing no one would miss him. Maybe she plans to feed me to them too!

Is that too evil? I think about this for a minute then decide that someone with hair like a numbat is probably capable of anything.

I imagine her strolling through the store after dark, calling to her pets and scattering meatpops for them like cat treats. *Here, little rat-slugs, come out my babies*. But it's not enough. Every now and again, they need fresh meat. Human meat.

The door handle rattles and I yelp. Quickly tossing

the filthy sausage roll back in with the others, I sit on my chair. This isn't good. Not good at all. I don't know how I'm meant to get out of this mess.

The door opens and there's Karen, grinning at me like *she's* the one who plans to eat me. I swallow heavily and make myself small. Only right then, there's a massive crash coming from somewhere in the warehouse. It's so loud I automatically clamp my hands over my ears.

"What is going on?" Karen screeches.

"Boss, there's been a disaster on aisle seventy-one," one of the twins cries, running over.

"The whole shelf has collapsed," the other one says.

Karen gasps. "Not the chandeliers!"

They run off down the main aisle. They've not gone far when a figure appears from the shadows and steps out in front of them.

"Is there a shop assistant who can help me with *this*?" Rube says, turning and waggling his bottom at them.

The twins gasp in unison.

"You little brat," Karen shouts. "Grab him!"

Rube shrieks as the three adults run towards him,

skidding on the shattered pieces of a chandelier. Rube's panicked yelling gets quieter and quieter as he sprints through the warehouse.

I stand in the doorway of the office, unsure what to do. I could run away, but what if that gets me into even *more* trouble? Like I said, breaking rules is a real problem for me.

Someone else makes up my mind for me. "Get her, quick!" a voice yells, and I'm picked up in a firefighter's lift and carried away.

THE GREAT FLATPACK TROLLY RACE

Emily has me slung over her shoulder. I wiggle but she's really strong. In the end, I give up and let her carry me. A minute later, she plonks me on to one of those big flat trolleys used for carrying bulky items.

"Go, go," she shouts at Ada and Jack. They run over to a second trolley.

Emily pushes our trolley and it immediately accelerates to a hair-raising speed. I have to cling on to stop myself from tipping off.

"What are you doing?" I say.

Emily is already sprinting at full speed through the

warehouse. "Rescuing you," she says. "We overheard Karen talking to those twins. She was planning to murder you or something."

"No, I'm sure she … watch out for the boxes!"

She swerves at the last minute, but we still collide with one of the boxes and packing material flies everywhere.

"Faster, let's goooo!" Jack shouts into his camera.

Jack's sitting on the second trolley, being pushed by Ada. He bounces into the air every time the trolley hits a bump. He slides around as she weaves past baskets of beach tents.

"We can beat them," he says, jiggling up and down like that's going to make Ada run faster. Her cheeks are red, and her face is set with determination.

"Why are we on trolleys?" I say in disbelief. "It would be faster to run."

"Stop complaining and make yourself more aerodynamic," Emily says, gritting her teeth.

"This is so dangerous!" I scream, as Emily abruptly turns a corner and pushes me down aisle twelve. I nearly slip off the trolley and have to kick off a shelf to stop myself from falling.

"We can't let Ada beat us," Emily says.

"When did this become a competition?" I shout. "I thought it was a rescue."

"You let yourself be captured. Rookie error," Jack says, as Ada swerves her trolley ahead of us. "Yes, we're winning!"

"I thought Karen would call my parents," I say. "Instead, she monologued her entire criminal plan at me."

"And now she has no choice except to murder us," Jack says. "Bummer."

"Ada, watch out for the patio umbrellas!" I shout.

Ada doesn't watch out and her trolley crashes into the box. The massive umbrellas all roll across the floor. Emily weaves through them and takes the lead again. She skids around a corner and heads straight for the flexible doors that lead into the public collection area. I shield my face and scream as we burst through. Ada is paces behind us.

"Faster," Jack shouts. "Come on, Ada. First Emily

steals your best friend and now she's going to beat you in a race."

I look back at him agog. He's such an unbelievable stirrer. I can't believe he's winding Ada up like this, making her think that beating Emily in a race is what matters right now.

Ada pulls her trolley level with ours and we all charge towards one of the tills. It's blocked off by an extendable belt barrier that kind of looks like a finish line. Ada's eyes are fixed squarely ahead. She expertly steers the trolley through posters of the night sky in which the moon has been replaced by a glowing meatpop – only 75p!

Emily's breathing heavily, but she finds an extra burst of speed. I think she's going to win but right at that moment, a red-faced Rube bursts through a door with Karen and the twins right behind him.

"Why are you still in the warehouse?" he shouts. "You were meant to get away before I led them back down here!"

"Yeah, that was the plan," Emily says. "But something came up."

"Emily, turn!" I shout. We're heading straight for the twins.

Emily growls in irritation. Like, actually growls. I don't think she's going to back out of the race but, at the last moment, she tries to make a sharp turn. We slam into a huge basket of chocolate bars. The impact stops the trolley abruptly. Chocolate bars go flying everywhere, and I slide off on to my bum. The floor's slippery, so I skid for a few metres before coming to a painful halt.

Jack howls. That's when I realize Ada's trolley is heading straight for me. I think it's going to hit me. The look on Ada's face makes me think she *wants* to hit me.

"Ada, no," Jack yells.

She reluctantly swerves and the trolley tips on to two wheels. It hits a kids' play slide and somehow the trolley is launched into the air. It shouldn't be possible for something so heavy to become airborne, but it flies a surprisingly long way. Ada clings on to the handlebar and cycles her legs in the air. Jack clings on to the base and screams.

They fly past one of the meatpop-moon posters.

Even the adults chasing us pause and watch them, open-mouthed. Then gravity catches up with them and the trolley crashes back to the ground. Ada and Jack roll across the floor. I worry they're badly hurt, but both scramble to their feet.

"What are you waiting for?" Ada says. "Run!"

Rube vaults over the extendable barrier blocking off the till and catches up with Ada and Jack. They run off through the warehouse. Emily waits for me to get up off the floor and we go after them. Karen and the twins are arguing about how to undo the barrier, but when they see us running, they climb over it.

We dart down the aisle that leads to the staff lift and stairs – the ones that lead up to the showroom's sofa zone. Karen and the twins are right behind us. They're making awful noises with their lungs. I don't think exercise is their thing.

"Take … the … lift," Karen wheezes.

We charge up the stairs. The lift is slow. We're going to have a decent head start when we get to the next floor. Tripping out of the stairwell, we push through the staff only door and out into the sofa zone. We weave through all the chairs and sofas without slowing our pace. My legs are burning, but I can't let Karen catch me again.

"There's a hidden route into bedrooms from the dining-room zone," Ada says, sounding out of breath. "Let's find somewhere to hide."

Bedrooms used to be my favourite zone. Whenever I came here with my parents, I'd try to pick out the room I'd want to be my own. There are so many to choose from, all with different themes. Some are grown-up and boring. Others are kids' rooms, and they're always a lot more fun. Or they used to be right up until I was trapped here with a bunch of shadow monsters and three thieving store workers.

We slow to a jog and hurry through the sets. Jack gasps in delight when he sees all the bedrooms. "Let's pick a room, people. Sleepover time!"

"We're running away, remember?" I say.

"Yeah, only because you got yourself captured," Emily says. She shoots me a grumpy look.

"I didn't know Karen was going to be such a ... such a ... Karen. I thought she'd be better than whatever that *thing* was in the bathroom zone!"

"What thing?" Rube says.

"The real monster?" I glance over at Ada. "You didn't tell them?"

"We were too busy rescuing you. Quick, in here," Ada says.

We dash into a kids' pirate-themed room. The bed's a mid sleeper shaped like a boat. The space underneath is surrounded by a play tent decorated to look like it's made of wood, with waves splashing around the bottom.

We crawl into the tent and pull the flaps closed. Without our torches, it's completely dark. Everyone is breathing fast after all the running.

"What did you mean, the real monster?" Rube whispers.

"*Shush*, we don't want Karen to find us," Emily says.

We all fall quiet again. There's no noise outside. I don't think Karen and the twins have come this way. Maybe they're following the Pink Brick Road in their hunt for us. Maybe they've had to stop for a little rest on one of the sofas.

"It was the ugliest thing I've ever seen," Ada whispers. "It was fantastic."

"It was half-slug, half-rat," I add.

"I tried to take a photo, but it didn't come out very well." She shows us her phone. It lights up the inside of the tent with a faint glow. The photo is rubbish. I can just about make out long yellow teeth and tiny black eyes.

"It looks like a naked mole rat," Rube says.

"Yeah, except it didn't have back legs," Ada said. "Its bum was like a giant slug."

"Wait, how big was this thing?" Emily says.

"Like an overweight guinea pig," Ada says. "Pretty small."

"I could drop-kick a guinea pig to the moon. To think we were scared," muses Emily.

"We?" Ada says, smirking. "I wasn't scared."

"Yeah, me neither," Emily says quickly.

"We should remember they're unfeasibly strong," Rube says. "One of them nearly dragged Jack away."

"They did drag Marcus Knight away," I add. "About that. I think Karen knows what happened to him. I think maybe she fed him to the creatures."

We all go quiet as this sinks in. Which proves to be a good thing. A moment later, footsteps approach. Ada quickly turns off her phone screen, but Karen and the twins pass us by without stopping. We wait to see if they come back, but everything goes quiet again.

"What now?" Jack whispers, switching on his torch.

"Nothing's changed," Ada says. "We haven't got any believable evidence of the creatures yet and—"

"You're kidding, right?" I snap. "This is dangerous!"

"Changing the world is never simple," Ada replies.

"I don't want to change the world; I just don't want to be eaten," I say, my voice catching.

"No one's going to be eaten," Emily says. "Right?"

Ada seems to think about this, then shrugs. Her lack of answer doesn't fill me with confidence. "Let's recap what we know so far."

"It's clearly a creature unknown to science," Rube says. "You described something that's part rodent and part gastropod mollusc. Evolutionarily speaking, those branches are millions of years apart."

"I don't understand that, but it sounds clever," Jack says.

"The shadows are the fascinating part," Rube continues. "They seem to be able to change the shadows they cast to mimic our worst nightmares."

I chew my lip. I don't want to mention this part to the others, but all of the shadows are things from old films that have terrified me in the past. Dinosaurs tracking a bunch of kids through a kitchen. A hellhound chasing someone through a shop. A spider silhouetted on a shower curtain.

The shadows are *my* worst nightmares, I realize.

"The important part," Ada says, "is that we now know what we're dealing with, so there's actually nothing to be scared of."

"I'm still pretty scared, if I'm honest," Jack says.

"Look, we've seen the creatures and we know how small they are. We can jump on to a chair and they won't be able to get us." Ada says this so confidently that, like usual, everyone believes she's right.

I find I don't have the energy to argue. I rest my head against the tent's frame and close my eyes. Tiredness catches up with me and, within minutes, I'm dreaming of the darkness of the forest.

STUMPY, BITER AND PINKY

A *scritch, scritch, scratch* drags me out of my dreams. Everyone has gone dead still. Their torches are all off, so the only illumination comes from the security lights, and they're not doing much to brighten the inside of this tent.

I straighten out my neck with a wince of pain. *Scritch, scritch, scratch*, comes the noise. It was scary enough when it was Karen hunting us. But I'd take her over these shadow monsters, no matter what Ada says. I don't care that they're small. Viruses are even smaller, and we're still scared of them.

"It can't get in, right?" Jack whispers, shuffling back from the zipped-up tent flaps.

"Maybe we should let it in and then we can catch it," Ada says.

"No!" I say quickly, then remember we're whispering. "Please don't," I add more quietly.

"All right, all right." Ada holds up her hands in defeat but looks pretty disappointed about it.

The scratching comes again. This time, it sounds like someone dragging their fingernails over fabric. There's a smell too. The woods after it's rained.

"They're back, aren't they?" Emily says wearily.

"*Shush*," Ada replies, readying her camera. "No one say anything."

Claws drag across the thin plastic tent. *Tap, tap, tapping* like it's feeling for a weakness in the fabric. I shuffle closer to Rube's end of the tent. So do all the others. We press ourselves together tightly, as far from the entrance as possible.

Scritch, scritch. Tap, tap.

Jack whimpers, his breath warm against my face. A shadow rises outside the tent. It has huge jaws and a rounded snout. A long body covered in bumpy scales and short, muscular legs. A crocodile.

Oh no. I know exactly where this fear came from, and it's embarrassing.

"*Peter Pan*," I whisper. "It's the crocodile that ate Captain Hook's hand."

"I'm not scared of the *Peter Pan* crocodile," Emily mutters. "Just saying."

"I'm not sure anyone over the age of seven is," Jack replies, laughing.

"Crocodiles are one of the only animals that survived the asteroid that wiped out the dinosaurs," Rube says. "The saltwater crocodile's bite is three times as strong as a lion's. And—"

"It's not a real crocodile," Ada interrupts. "It's a small rodent of some kind, with a big shadow."

"Small rodent" doesn't quite do it justice. I remember its horrible slimy tail and all the wonky teeth. And the way it almost managed to drag Jack away, despite being so tiny.

The claws scrabble at the entrance into the tent. The crocodile shadow looms.

"What are we going to do?" I say, my voice shaking.

"We need to get off the ground," Emily says. "We

wait until the creature moves away from the flaps, then we burst out making as much noise as possible and get up on to the bed."

"What if it attacks?" Jack says.

Emily picks up a plastic sword from a box of books and toys stored under the bed. "It won't dare," she says.

The scrabbling stops. We all hold our breath. Then the edge of the tent nearest to me twitches and a small paw with massive claws sneaks underneath. I can see the outline of the creature's face pressed up against the fabric. Its mouth is open wide and its sharp teeth are threatening to puncture the material. Screaming, I scramble over the others and fumble with the zip.

"I guess we're going then," Ada says.

We crawl out of the tent in a big tangle of arms and legs. I push myself off the nearest person, barely registering Jack's yelp of surprise. Then I clamber up the ladder leading to the deck of the boat, AKA the bed. I curl up in the corner, as far away from the ladder as I can.

"It's got me, it's got me!" Rube screams.

He grabs the bedframe and clings on. The creature

has hold of his trousers and is trying to drag him away. It's even uglier than I remember from the bathroom set. Its skin is all white and wrinkled, like your toes when you stay in the bath too long.

Its teeth are yellow and stick out in every direction. Its tiny eyes are gummy round the edges, like it has a bad allergy to something.

"Don't you dare," Emily says, swinging the pirate sword at the rat-slug. It goes flying, and its massive, impossible crocodile shadow disappears. The creature slaps into the side of a bookcase with a moist sound. Then it tumbles to the ground and scuttles into a tiny gap beneath a chest of drawers.

"It's a wall tumbler," Jack says, with awe.

"A what?" Ada says.

"You know, those toys made of squashy stuff, and you can throw them at a wall?"

"That's a sticky splat," Emily says.

"Get up on the bed!" I shout. "Before it comes back."

They all stop arguing and quickly climb the ladder. They're just in time. A second creature – and I know it's not the same one because it's pink and has a tuft of hair on the top of its head – scurries around the corner and tries to bite Emily's shoe. She kicks it away and it runs for the shadows.

"Wow, these things are hideous!" Emily says, pulling her legs on to the bed.

"I think they're adorable," Rube says. He notices our horrified stares. "I mean, all nature's creatures are special in their own way. Obviously, they're not going to be featured on the front cover of a magazine anytime soon."

"It's impossible to take their picture anyway," Ada says, glaring at her phone. "The shadows look like ordinary shadows; it's so annoying."

"What I want to know is how are they changing their shadows?" Jack says. "I'm no physics professor, but I'm pretty sure shadows don't work that way."

"I don't know if they are changing their shadows," Rube says, looking thoughtful. "Maybe they're making us think they're changing their shadows."

"Er … what?" Emily says.

Rube roots in his bag and pulls out the clicky device he showed us earlier. "Whenever they're close, I detect electromagnetic fluctuations. Lots of people think human consciousness is a result of the brain's electromagnetic field. My theory is, the creatures communicate by electromagnetic radiation. It's not impossible they're using this to put thoughts into our heads."

"Like telepathy?" I say.

"Exactly. And I think it works the other way too. If I'm correct, they can *hear* our fears, and they're using them against us," he says.

I pull a face. If that's true, then it must sound like I'm screaming at the top of my lungs. No wonder it seems to be my fears the shadow monsters are picking up on. I'm hit by a rush of shame. Maybe if I wasn't so scared, they'd leave us alone. I'm the weakest link, the member of the group they've homed in on as easy prey.

"Look, there's another one," Jack says.

I catch a flash of a short, rounded tail as a creature dives under a wardrobe. This one is much moister than the other two. Under the security lights, it gleams wetly.

"Interesting," Rube says. "I think he lost his tail at some point and has regrown it like a lizard. It's definitely stumpier than the others."

"I'm going to call him Stumpy," Jack says. "The first

one is now named Biter, for obvious reasons. And the girl can be called Pinky."

"The girl?" Emily says. "You're presuming it's a girl because it's pink?"

I glance between Jack and Emily. Jack's wearing much more pink than she is. In fact, the closest to pink on her is the dark purple stripe in her hair, dyed for a recent football tournament. In comparison, Jack is wearing pale pink trousers and bright pink nail polish.

"You have a valid point." He grins at her. "But she was fast, right?"

Emily sniffs in what I think is begrudging agreement.

They're naming the creatures that want to eat us instead of trying to find a way to escape. Unbelievable. I turn my attention to the rest of the bedroom zone, trying to work out how we're going to get out of this mess.

That's when I spot a flight of stairs a few sets over. The space underneath has been converted into a little reading nook full of beanbags, cushions and a book trolley. The stairs themselves stop abruptly and lead nowhere. But I think we could use them to climb on to the beams above the set.

I'm not a big fan of heights, but those beams criss-cross the entire showroom. We could use them to go anywhere. We could use them to get out of here. Most importantly, Stumpy, Biter and Pinky won't be able to reach us.

"I have a plan," I tell the others.

THE FLOOR IS LAVA

"The floor is lava," I say.

"Are the monsters not *enough*?" Jack says.

"No, I mean the game. If we stay off the floor and move quickly, I don't think they'll be able to get us."

Emily rubs her hands together. "I am amazing at this, just so you know."

"We need to get across to that set in the corner, with the flight of stairs at the back. See it?" I point across the zone.

"Easy," Emily says.

She crawls to the edge of the bed, crouches, then jumps with her arms and legs outstretched. Pretending to be a flying squirrel wasn't exactly what I had in mind when I suggested this plan. She makes it though, landing heavily on a chest of drawers.

The drawers aren't so lucky. The wood makes a loud cracking noise and everything on top topples to the floor. A whale-shaped lamp smashes. A row of books fall like dominoes. Emily doesn't seem to notice she's destroying the set.

"Come on then," she says, glancing back at us. "What are you waiting for?"

"I don't think I can do that," Rube says. "I'm still recovering from leading Karen and her minions on a chase round half the store."

"You're the one who volunteered," Ada says unsympathetically.

"Err, yes," he says, "because I didn't want anyone to think I only bring animal facts to the table. I'm a man of many talents, although maybe running isn't one of them."

My tummy sinks. If Rube is worried he's not doing enough to help the group, then what must they all think about me? I don't think I've contributed anything useful at all. All I've done is get scared and get captured.

"Climb down on to that beanbag," Emily says. "It's an easier route."

Rube goes first, unsteadily balancing on the beanbag, then letting Emily help him up on to the chest of drawers. Jack follows, then Ada. It bothers me that, even dressed in an impractical unicorn onesie, Ada doesn't struggle in the slightest. She jumps on to a coffee table with a swish of her rainbow tail.

"Olive?" she says. "Are you coming this way or what?"

I shake my head and force a smile. "No, I'm good. I have a route planned out."

I don't have a route planned out. Although this was my idea, I'm not great at this sort of thing. I'm way too clumsy. But I don't want them thinking I need someone to hold my hand all the time. Like Rube, I feel as if I have something to prove.

I slide over the edge of the bed and down on to a child-sized armchair. If I can make it to the other side of the pirate bedroom, I can climb through a little fake window into the neighbouring set. The route isn't as easy as the one the others are taking, but at least it's my own.

I teeter on the armchair. It's not as stable as I thought it would be. A scratching noise makes me nearly lose my balance, but I grab a bookcase and step on to the bottom shelf. I carefully edge across towards a wardrobe.

"Olive, you're not high enough!" Emily shouts.

I glance behind me. The first thing I see is the shadow. It's not a dinosaur or a hellhound or a crocodile. No, it's a literal volcano, spewing out lava. I've been terrified of volcanoes ever since my dads showed me a nineties film in which someone's feet melted in a lake of magma. Volcanoes are in my top five fears, even though I live in a geologically stable country.

"Olive!" Rube shouts. "Your feet."

For a second, I panic I'm going to lose my feet to a pool of hot lava. But no, it's Biter. Despite already knowing what he looks like, his appearance still makes me squeal in horror. It's the teeth, and the soulless black eyes, and everything else about him.

"Jack," Ada says. "You need to be filming this. I don't have a good angle."

"On it," Jack says.

Biter jumps up and nips at my ankle. His horrible

yellow teeth rip into the fabric of my leggings. At first there's a gentle tug, then a violent yank. How is something so small that strong?

"It's going to Marcus her," Jack cries, fumbling his camera.

The thought of being dragged off and never seen again gives me a burst of strength. I grab a book off the upper shelf and throw it at Biter. The book whacks him on the nose and he relaxes his grip long enough for me to shake my leg free.

I reach over towards the wardrobe, but the door swings open and I find myself dangling from it. Biter jumps up at me, gnashing his wonky teeth as the door swings back and forth. I manage to grab the window frame mid-swing. I kick off the wardrobe and heave myself headfirst through the small square. It's not dignified, but I don't care.

"Please say you got a shot of him," Ada says.

"Sorry," Jack says. "I think I forgot to press record."

"One job," Ada grumbles.

The others go back to their journeys across the zone. I try to pull myself through the hole, but my bum's wedged. I dangle half through with my arms and legs waggling. "I'm stuck," I call out.

They stop and look back. They're all in a neighbouring set already, not far from the bedroom with the staircase. I, on the other hand, have chosen a route that will take me twice as long. All because I was trying to prove I'm not a complete disaster.

"What on Earth were you thinking?" Emily shouts. "That hole is tiny."

"Bones," Rube says. "You have bones, Olive."

"Yes, I know." I brace myself against the flimsy wall. It wobbles, but I can't get through the window. The sill digs into my belly.

"Try twerking," Jack says. "Twerk like your life depends on it."

I give it a go, but all it does is violently shake the wall. Books and toys fall off the shelves. Jack cracks up with laughter. "I didn't think you'd do that. I wish I'd recorded you."

"Wait, I have a sandwich in my bag." Rube balances on a bedside table and tries to reach into his backpack.

"I don't think a snack is going to help," I say.

"Butter," he says. "We can smear you in butter."

"No! I don't need to be smeared in butter," I shout. I think I'd rather be eaten than suffer the humiliation. "I'm sure I can get out by myself."

The next set is a safari-themed bunkbed room. I can

reach the bedframe. I use it to slowly – and painfully – pull myself through the hole. Suddenly, my hips are free and I slither out, crashing on to a beanbag. Before anything can get me, I climb on to the upper bunk. The others all cheer.

"Get lost," I grumble, trying to ignore their laughter.

I look for my next move. I'm going to have to make a run for the set on the opposite side of the Pink Brick Road. There's no sign of the creatures, so I should make it in time.

Before I can gather the courage, I hear Jack screaming. He's crouching on a swivel chair right in the middle of the path. I think he must have tried to push himself over to another set. Two of the creatures are advancing on him, their claws scratching at the floor and their bums making horrible squelchy noises. Their shadows are huge, lumbering monsters. Lava monsters, I realize.

"They're coming for me," he yells. "Someone help me."

"You're fine, they can't reach you," Ada says. "Push off quickly and wheel away."

Jack kicks off the floor, but he gets the angle wrong. He ends up spinning further into the no man's land between sets. The creatures crawl closer. Biter chomps one of the wheels on the chair, making Jack shriek even louder.

"Kick it away," Emily says. "It's tiny."

"No, they're really strong," I shout. "Don't let it grab you."

Proving my point, Biter starts to drag the chair – and Jack – away. I'm not sure where it's taking him, but I don't think it will be somewhere good.

"Help me, help me," Jack screams, bouncing on the chair like he's desperate for a wee.

Emily makes a displeased sniffing noise, then climbs down on to the floor and runs out into the open. "Oi, little monsters. Come and eat me!"

Pinky looks up. She breaks away from tormenting Jack and rushes towards Emily. She moves with surprising speed, given the fact she's shaped like a squashed cushion with two arms and a face. Emily's faster, though. She clambers on to a sofa.

She throws one end of a knitted blanket at Jack.

"Grab hold! I'll pull you over here."

He does what he's told, but Biter isn't giving up easily. He yanks at the chair. Emily yanks at the blanket. Jack does a lot of screaming. Finally, Biter realizes he's beaten and releases Jack. The chair flies towards Emily, colliding with her sofa and tipping over. Jack flies off and nearly flattens Emily, but they're both safe.

While the shadow creatures are distracted, Ada and Rube hurry across the Pink Brick Road. They climb on to an armchair, then jump over on to the sofa. I'm still the only one on the wrong side of the zone. It's hard to make myself move, though.

"Come on, Olive," Emily says. "Hurry up."

Taking a deep breath, I climb halfway down the bunkbed ladder. I jump the rest of the way and make a run for it. The room opposite me is set up with an old-fashioned Christmas morning scene, despite Christmas being many months away. I plan to climb on to the bed, with its green and red cushions. I don't make it, though. Stumpy is too fast.

He scuttles towards me and I have to jump on to an old-fashioned rocking horse. It has a big wooden base and is painted dappled grey and white. Its wooden teeth aren't much straighter than Stumpy's.

"Yes, come on. You've got this," Emily says, clapping her hands like she's encouraging her football team.

I've clearly *not* got this.

"Jump over to the bookcase already," Ada says.

I try to make myself jump, I really do, but the horse starts to rock beneath me. I cling on to its mane with both hands. It rocks again, even harder, even faster. I glance down. Stumpy and Pinky have hold of the rockers. They're tilting the horse violently in an attempt to shake me off.

I want to close my eyes and bury my face in the horse's mane. My heart is beating at a million beats a minute and I can hardly catch my breath. But if I don't move, the creatures are going to tip me off on to the floor and drag me away.

"I'm going to count you down," Emily says. "Three … two…"

She doesn't get to finish because I fall off the horse. The creatures scuttle towards me, but I manage to dive into a bargain bin full of stuffed giraffes. I sink into the fluffiness and it's actually quite comfortable.

Then something grabs me from underneath. It yanks on my leg and pulls me down, beneath the surface. I try to claw my way to the top, but whoever it is – Biter, I think – is ridiculously strong.

I can't see anything. The fur of the toys tickles my nose and eyes. I want to scream, but there's no air. I'm going to suffocate and there's nothing I can do to save myself.

BIRD'S-EYE VIEW

Arms heave me out of the basket. I land in a heap and gasp in lungfuls of air. Even though I'm not in the basket any more, I feel like the world is pressing in on me.

"It got hold of me," I sob. "It got me."

"What got you?" Emily says, eyeing the basket of giraffes.

I realize I'm on the floor and I start to panic in case one of the creatures grabs me again. Scrambling on to a bed, I tuck my legs up.

"They're gone," Ada says, sighing. "They heard

something and took off. I still didn't manage to get a single clear photo."

"The electromagnetic radiation they use to communicate is probably interfering with the camera," Rube says.

"What did they hear?" I ask, still nervously looking around. Something must have scared them off.

"Oh, it's Karen again," Jack says casually. "She's coming this way with those twins. It sounds like they're moving furniture."

"Karen's coming this way?" I say. "Now?"

We all stare at each other in silence, then everyone bolts for the fake staircase. We clamber over the plastic barrier that's supposed to stop people from climbing the stairs. Emily pulls herself on to one of the ceiling beams and helps me up after her. All my limbs instantly go wobbly. It's so high.

"Crawl that way," Emily whispers.

"I don't know if I can," I reply. If I move even an inch, I'm sure I'll fall. When I came up with this idea, I thought my fear of the rat-slugs would override my fear of heights. Nope.

"You can do it," Rube says. "Imagine you're a goat. You wouldn't think goats are good at climbing, but actually—"

"No time for goats," Ada says. "Move, Olive, or we're going to get caught."

I slowly shuffle along the beam on my bum. All my muscles are tensed. My hands are shaking. I make it to a criss-cross on which I can balance, which gives Ada, Rube and Jack enough room to climb up behind me. We all perch there like birds as Karen walks right beneath us. If she even looks up a little bit, she's going to see us. She doesn't look up, though. She's too busy shouting orders at the twins, who are struggling to carry a bookcase between them.

"Come on," she complains.

"What are they doing?" Emily mouths at me.

I shrug and watch as the men shove the bookcase into the secret path between bedrooms and outdoor furniture. I don't think they're stealing stock any more. This is something else.

"Get that passageway sealed off," Karen says. "Hurry up."

The twins screw the wardrobe to the partition walls with a noisy electric screwdriver.

"Those brats aren't going to escape this time," Karen mutters.

She draws a large cross on a store map. I can't quite see the whole thing clearly from this height, but it looks like they're sealing up various routes through the store.

"What's the plan again?" one of the twins asks. "I'm confused."

Karen makes an exasperated noise and tilts her head to the ceiling. I grimace, but luckily she has her eyes closed and doesn't see us up here. "We've been through this. We're going to chase them into living-rooms and make sure all their escape routes are blocked off. The only way for them to go will be down the old stairs into Warehouse Two."

"Those stairs are stinky," the other twin says.

"Warehouse Two is stinky," his brother adds. "All the smelly furniture gets put down there. It's disgusting."

Karen glares at him. "That's the point," she says. "Nobody goes down there unless it's to drop off an infested item."

"But the kids are going to go down there?"

"Yes! Haven't you listened to anything I've told you? We're going to prop open the door leading to Warehouse Two, the kids will go down the stairs and, once we have them trapped ... well, let's say I'm looking forward to that part."

The twin with a screwdriver pats the bookcase. "All done, boss. Do you want us to dress it? A couple of pineapples and some books, yeah?"

"Urgh, leave it." She clicks her fingers at them. "Let's go."

They move across to the other side of the zone. I can hear them dragging furniture around.

"I don't like the sound of Warehouse Two," Emily says.

"I think they were talking about the stairs we found earlier," I say. "Remember when we got behind the scenes in the dining-room zone, and it smelt really bad? There was a stairwell down there."

"The one you wouldn't let me explore," Jack says, pouting at me.

"What Karen and her goons don't realize is that we

don't need passageways to move around any more," Ada says, patting the beam we're balanced on. "Now we can safely track the shadow monsters *and* avoid those fools."

Nothing fazes her, it's infuriating. We have a store worker with a grudge hunting us down, and a bunch of hungry critters trying to drag us to our deaths. Any reasonable person would be cutting their losses and trying to escape the store. Instead, she's still charging on ahead with her original plan.

"I want to go home," I say abruptly. Admitting this out loud feels ... good. Freeing.

"You can't go home," Ada snaps. "Not when we're so close to getting our proof."

"Except we're not close," I say. "Every time we encounter those creatures, someone nearly dies."

"No one's come even close to dying," she scoffs, rolling her eyes.

"I was seconds away from suffocation."

"You fell in a basket of giraffes and couldn't get out. It wasn't that dramatic."

"It felt dramatic to me!"

"Everything feels dramatic to you, Olive."

Emily, Jack and Rube all suck in a sharp intake of breath. Ada stares at me with her chest heaving and her nostrils flaring. Beneath her unicorn hood, her eyes gleam with anger. I open my mouth to argue, but no words come out. So instead, I clamber along the beam as fast as my shaky arms and wobbly legs will take me.

The outdoor-furniture section is the last zone in the showroom, so I head in that direction. From there, I can get to the canteen and find a fire exit. Sure, opening it will set off all the alarms and summon the police and the fire department. We'll get in loads of trouble, but it's better than staying here a moment longer.

"Olive, wait," Emily says. "Where are you going?"

"I'm going to get help," I say, and to my shame, my voice comes out shaky like I'm going to cry. "I want to go home."

I hear the others whispering among themselves. They can think what they want of me, but I know I am being completely reasonable for once. A bunch of weird naked rat-slugs tried to drag us away. Weird naked rat-slugs with shadows that look like my worst nightmares. Anyone who *doesn't* want to go home after all that is the unreasonable one.

I reach the bed and mattress zone. It's set out like a massive dormitory. There are rows and rows of various beds with different mattresses so shoppers can test them all out before making their choice. From above, it looks like a big maze.

"Olive, stop," Ada says. She's walking on one of the beams, going dangerously fast in an attempt to cut me off. Her head is dipped and her unicorn horn points menacingly at me.

"Get out of my way," I say.

"No, I'm not letting you ruin this for me!"

"It's all about you, isn't it?" I yell, surprising myself.

I never lose my temper but I can't hold the anger inside any more. It's not just the danger we're all in. It's everything. All the times Ada told me what to do. All the times she embarrassed me. All the times she insisted on doing what *she* wanted to do without thinking about me. The fact that she didn't even try to fight for our friendship. She replaced me with Rube like I meant nothing to her.

"What are you talking about?" she says, rolling her eyes again.

"You want to make yourself look good, even if it puts the rest of us in danger. You're so obsessed with finding proof of your monsters that you don't care about anyone else."

"I never asked you to come here with me," she says.

"I didn't want to come here!"

"And yet here you are, following your new friends like a little *sheep*. You're so desperate for them to like you, it's pathetic."

"Stop, both of you," Rube pleads, trying to shush us.

But I can't stop. Now my anger has started to come out, it won't stop.

"*I'm* pathetic?" I cry. "You're the one who doesn't let anyone else have a say in anything. It's always the Ada show."

"Maybe you don't have anything interesting to say. You don't ever *do* anything, Olive. You just complain!"

"Ada, that's enough," Emily says.

"Please stop shouting for a second and listen to me," Rube pleads. "You need to listen to me."

"Were we *ever* friends?" I ask Ada. "Because it felt like you didn't even like me. You wanted someone to carry your stuff and agree with all your schemes."

"Yeah, that's exactly what it was," she shouts. "Why would I want to be friends with you?"

I nod slowly. It's weird. She's gone all twitchy and red in the face, like she's about to explode. Whereas I feel like time is moving so slowly I can see it flowing around me. It's a brief moment of peace. The eye of the storm.

"Olive!" Rube cries. "Watch out for Mr Sticky!"

I snap out of my trance and look down in time to see Karen swinging her pole at me and knocking me off the beam.

WE'RE GONNA
A BIGGER BED

I land on my back, on a soft mattress that feels like a big marshmallow. Rube quickly follows, and I have to roll aside to avoid becoming *his* soft landing.

"Get down from there, right now," Karen orders, whacking Jack with Mr Sticky.

"Ouch, that hurts! Watch my jacket, it's real velvet!" Jack cries. He dangles from the overhead beam, kicking his legs.

Ada and Emily both slide off their own beans, using two headboards to safely climb down. Jack isn't quite so graceful. He falls and lands on an expensive mattress that bounces him straight back into the air.

"I'm flying!" He windmills his arms and legs, then face plants on to another mattress. "Oof."

"Grab them!" Karen pulls some cable ties out of her pocket and lunges at me.

Screaming, I scramble over a squeaky leather headboard, on to the bed on the opposite side. This mattress is wrapped in plastic, and it slips under my feet.

"Stop moving," one of the twins complains, as Emily ducks under his huge arms and rolls across a bed. "Stay still and let me tie you up."

"Let me think about that," Emily says. "Um, it's a no."

Karen slaps aside a cardboard sign announcing twenty per cent off memory-foam pillows. She marches towards me. Her face is red with fury. "Get off that bed with your dirty shoes. Now."

Emily jumps on to the bed next to me and takes my hand. "Bounce, Olive!"

She pulls me with her and I have no choice but to jump between the beds, faster and faster. I constantly feel on the cusp of falling over. Then we step on to a squishy memory-foam mattress and we do fall over.

The bed's so soft it's a struggle to get back up, but we've put some distance between us and Karen. She's trying to use the paths between the beds to reach us, and that means walking up and down each aisle.

Both twins are trying to catch Jack, but he keeps bouncing from bed to bed. He looks like he's having fun, recording their furious shouts as they try to snatch him out of the air. "Too slow," he taunts, then screams as one of the men almost grabs him by the ankle.

Rube and Ada catch up with me and Emily. "Get to the next zone," Ada orders. "We can hide from them in there."

Jack runs past us, stepping between the beds with his arms flailing. "I can't slow down, I'm going too fast," he shouts.

We go after him, but that's when I catch sight of a shadow out of the corner of my eye. It slides across a white headboard and briefly vanishes. Then it's back, this time on a poster of a woman floating in the ocean on a mattress.

The shadow's a shark's dorsal fin. It swims past the woman on the poster, then disappears. Claws scuttle against the laminate floor. I can't see the creatures, but I know they're somewhere under the beds.

"They're here!" I shout. "Stay off the ground, they're here!"

"Who's here?" Jack looks at me as he bounces and misjudges his landing. With a yelp, he topples off the bed and lands with a thud. "I'm fine," he says, groaning.

"Get back on the bed," I yell at him. "The shadow monsters are here."

There's a rapid scurrying noise and Jack screams. Emily and I reach him just in time and heave him out of danger. A pale pink blur flashes past and vanishes under the next bed.

The distraction has allowed Karen and the twins to catch up. They're trying to cut off our escape routes, I realize. They advance towards us with their chests heaving from all the exercise. Karen, in particular, looks like she could use a nap in one of the beds.

"This way," Rube says.

I follow him on to a simple metal-frame bed. But as I land, the bed jumps beneath me. I hold on to a bedknob to steady myself. "What was that?" I whisper.

The bed bumps again, lifting all the way off the ground. I lose my balance and end up lying on my tummy with my head dangling off the bed. For a second, I see underneath. Stumpy stares back at me from a metre away, with his yellow teeth bared. He flies at my face and I barely avoid being mauled.

On another bed, Jack is clinging on for his life. The bed bucks up and down as the creature underneath tries to shake him off. "Why are they so strong?" he says.

"It's common in the animal kingdom," Rube replies. "The Rhinoceros Beetle can lift eight hundred and fifty times its own weight. That's like me picking up a humpback whale."

"Why would you want to lift a humpback whale?" Emily says.

"If I could lift a whale, I'd be doing it all the time," Jack says. "Everyone would be like, here comes Jack with his whale again. He's so amazing." His bed tips and he makes a desperate leap to safety.

"And did you know, snails have teeth made of the strongest substance on the planet?" Rube continues, then stops talking when the bed we're on starts to shake violently.

"Keep moving," Ada says. "We can't stay in one place for too long."

We try to bounce faster, but the creatures can flit from beneath one bed to another several metres away in a split-second.

"I think they're teleporting," Rube says. "It's how they get about."

"If I'm right, then they can travel between any dark

space," Ada shouts. "They could be anywhere."

As the creatures move, their shadows jump from wall to headboard, sign to bedside table. Dorsal fins glide past. Tails flick. Sharks erupt with their toothy mouths open wide. I know exactly where this fear is from – I watched *Jaws* last summer. But the scariest bit for me was when you *couldn't* see the shark. When it was right under the boat, readying itself for an attack.

We reach the edge of the zone and it's only then I notice it's been blocked off by two beds lifted on to their ends. We don't have time to move them. The creatures will attack if we try.

"Dead end," Emily shouts back to Rube, Jack and Ada. "We can't get through into the next zone!"

"That's because we've blocked it off, you terrors," Karen shouts. "We've got you now." She clicks her fingers at the twins and gestures for them to cut us off from the right.

We all bounce on to the same double bed and huddle together right in the centre, as far away as possible from all our pursuers – human and non-human. Karen and the twins grin as they get closer. The shadow sharks circle.

"Grab a cushion," Emily whispers. "They can't take us all on."

"But they can grab at least three of us," Jack says.

Ada glances between the rest of us. I know she's weighing up her chances of being one of the two who get away. Her odds are good, when it comes to Karen and the twins, at least. But they're not the only ones we have to worry about.

A bed behind Karen bumps. She glances back with a frown, but it's already fallen still. Another one jerks into the air, this one closer. "What is that?" Karen snaps.

I wince as another bed bounces, then another, and another. It's a ripple of beds being lifted into the air as the creatures rush straight for us.

"We're going to need a bigger bed," Jack says, squeezing me so tight I feel like I might pop. "Preferably one that weighs more than a humpback whale."

The bumping beds fall still. There's a horrible pause where the creatures, with their scrabbling claws, go completely silent. "You need to get to higher ground," I say to one of the twins.

He scratches his head. "Huh?"

Suddenly, his feet are yanked out from beneath him and he slams to the floor. He screams and claws his fingernails into the concrete, but the creature's too strong. It drags him under a bed and the screaming instantly stops. I think the creature's teleported him away, to another dark place.

"Bob? Bob!" his twin shouts.

"Wait, I thought you were Bob?" Karen says.

The man glances at his name badge. It definitely reads Bob. "Oh. We look identical so I can't tell the difference. Bill, where are you?"

"Seriously, get off the floor," I tell him.

It's too late. He too is yanked off his feet and dragged out of sight.

Karen looks around, puzzled. "What's going on?

What have you done to them?"

"It's not us," Rube says. "It's the creatures."

"You need to get on the bed," I say. "Or they'll get you too."

"What exactly is going to get me, young lady?" she snaps. "I hope you're not threatening me."

"Let her get eaten," Ada says. "It will be no loss."

"Eaten?" Karen barks, laughing nastily. "That's ridiculous."

"There are monsters living in this store," I plead. "They ate Marcus Knight."

"They ... Marcus?" She frowns and I realize my earlier presumption was wrong. She doesn't know about the creatures. They're not her pets.

"Careful, it's coming!" I say, as a bed lifts then drops back to the floor. Karen glances down at her feet. With a cry of alarm, she jumps on to a bed. "Urgh, there's a rat."

"It's not a rat," Rube says. "It's a species unknown to science."

"Don't be so ridiculous." Karen's bed bounces and she wails in anguish. "I hate rats!"

Her bed shakes faster and faster. She screams louder and louder and hugs the metal bars of the headboard. We all stand there watching, unsure what to do. On the one hand, I feel like we should be trying to help her. But then again, she's mean.

"Hey, where's Ada going?" Jack says.

Ada's used everyone's distraction to bounce away, and she's already halfway across the room. She's gone without us!

"Go!" Emily says. We take off after Ada as Karen's screaming crescendos. The creatures don't chase us – they're too busy trying to tip Karen on to the floor.

"Ada, slow down," Rube calls.

Ada glances back at us. "Nice of you to join me," she says.

"Why did you leave us?" he asks, sounding hurt.

"I didn't leave you," she says, rolling her eyes. She holds up her phone. "I was protecting my footage."

"Did you get them?" Jack says, quickly bouncing on to Ada's bed.

Ada grins smugly. "I got a good shot of Stumpy. It's going to make me famous."

"You say '*me*' like you were the only one risking your butt to get that footage," Emily says, folding her arms.

"The discovery is the important part," Ada says.

Anger gets hold of me again. She really is the most selfish person in the whole world. We nearly died, and all she is thinking about is herself. Before I can think about what I'm doing, I bounce to her and snatch the phone from her hand. I throw it as hard as I can across the zone. It hits a side-table and shatters into three pieces.

"Stop!" I shriek at her. "I've had enough!"

She stares at me like she doesn't recognize me. I'm not sure I recognize myself. "I can't believe you did that," she whispers. She jumps off the bed and runs towards the phone. The others all call out for her to stop, but she's not listening.

That's when I notice Karen is no longer screaming. Instead, she's backing away along the Pink Brick Road. Nothing is chasing her. I don't think the creatures want her. Only, if nothing's chasing her, that means...

"Get off the ground!" I yell at Ada, but it's too late.

She's yanked off her feet and lands on her belly with

a painful slapping noise. She reaches her hands out towards us as she's dragged under the bed. The last view I get of her is her unicorn horn disappearing out of sight. The shadows and Ada are gone. She's just gone.

GONE WITHOUT A TRACE

"Where is she?" Rube cries. "Ada? Ada!"

We kneel on the floor and look under all the beds. I have a clear view from one end of the zone to the other, broken only by bed legs and dust bunnies. There's no sign of her, or of the creatures that stole her away.

"They've taken her," Jack hiccups. "Like they took Marcus."

"OK, let's stay calm," Emily says. "We're going to get her back. It will be fine."

"How's it going to be fine?" I cry. "The police searched this place for Marcus and they never found him. They won't find Ada either."

Minutes ago, I was thinking about escaping. But now that option is gone. I can't leave the store and risk no one believing our story. If someone doesn't find Ada soon, she'll be lost forever.

"We have to find her ourselves," I say, breaking into a run. I burst into the bedroom zone with the others close behind me. Sudden scuttling noises make me spin around. The shadows move too fast for me to make them out. By the time I look at them, they're already vanishing out of sight.

"Wait, I think we need a plan," Rube says.

Usually, it's me telling everyone we need a plan. But Ada's been taken and it's my fault! I can't stop and plan. Every second matters.

"Look everywhere," I say. "The creatures can jump between dark spaces, so she could be anywhere."

"Ada?" Jack cries, pulling a wardrobe door open and looking inside. "Where are you?"

Another scuttling sound leads me deeper into the bedroom sets. The shadows dart past, melting into dark corners and then reappearing somewhere else a split-second later. I try to follow them, thinking they'll lead me to Ada. They're always gone before I can get there.

"Come back," I shout. "Give Ada back!"

"Slow down," Emily pleads. "I think we need to search properly."

But I can't slow down. "Over there!" I shout. "I think I saw Pinky."

We all run to the pirate bedroom where we encountered the crocodile shadow earlier. I yank open the wardrobe; Jack looks under the bed. We shine our torches into all the dark places, but there's no sign of Ada or the creatures.

"Why do they keep vanishing?" I cry.

"Why aren't they attacking?" Rube says. "I think we should stop and talk about this. Something's different."

"They're taunting us!" I say. "They've taken Ada and now they're laughing at us."

I see a glimpse of a shadow and run along the secret path leading through to the dining-room zone. I shine my torch under the tables and into every cupboard. But she's not here.

"Ada!" I shout. "Where are you?"

I can't stop thinking about how I argued with her

right before she was stolen away. All the horrible things we said to each other could end up being our last conversation. Her final memory of me will be me accusing her of turning everything into the Ada show.

It's true she's always at the centre of everything, but that's because she does things that matter. Interesting things. I've always loved that about Ada. She cares about stuff and stands up for what she believes in. Somewhere along the way, I forgot all the good things about her. I was too busy feeling angry because she sometimes gets over-excited and doesn't stop to ask how I'm feeling. But now she's in trouble, all my anger feels pointless. I just want my friend back.

I run out into the kitchen zone. I'm always one step behind the creatures. I spot a flash of movement reflected in a chrome surface. A shadow flits across tiles. I can never catch up, no matter how fast I run.

"Ada?" I shout. "Where are you?"

My heart is beating so fast. I worry I'm going to be sick. I know I need to breathe steadily and take a moment to calm myself. But there's no time.

The others catch me up. They call for me to wait,

to slow down and think for a minute. But I'm already running for the living-room zone. I'm not searching for her methodically, I know that. I'm panicking too much.

On the other side of the zone, I spot an open door that wasn't there before. A partition wall has been removed and it's lying on the floor. I know this door. It's the same one Jack, Emily and I found earlier, when we went behind the scenes. This has to be the staircase down into Warehouse Two.

Karen's trap for us.

The shadows slide into the darkness beyond the door. It's not just Karen's trap, I realize. The monsters have led us here and now they're waiting for us. Ada's the bait and we're supposed to follow.

I walk towards the top of the stairs, but my legs are sluggish. As I get closer, I can smell the damp and the rot. I stop.

"That's where they've taken her, isn't it?" Jack says. "Because of course it is."

Emily peers down into the stairwell. "All right, we're going to need weapons," she says.

"What if it's a trap?" Rube says.

I'm sure it *is* a trap. But we can't leave Ada down there, alone in the darkness. I have to be brave. I have to get my fear under control. I can't... I can't...

Even now my best friend is in trouble, I can't make myself go down that staircase. Ada was right. When have I ever *done* anything? I follow others and do what I'm told. Now that Ada needs me, I'm too scared to try to help her.

With a noisy sob, I turn away from the door leading down to Warehouse Two and I run away.

EVERYONE GETS SCARED

I run and run, wishing I could leave everything behind.
But I can't get away from myself. The problem is me.
And my fear. It gets in the way of everything. Making
friends, talking to people, saving Ada.

Sometimes I think of my fear as a big scary monster
that lives inside my head. Anytime I think about trying
something new, it's the monster that tells me I can't. He
keeps reminding me of all the bad things that might
happen, like getting hurt or having people laugh at me.
He's always there, whispering to me.

When I imagine what he looks like, he's this big
black cloud with a million spidery legs. The legs reach

into every part of me. They're all tangled up with every thought I've ever had. He's there even in the good thoughts, whispering that maybe they're not real. I can't run away from him because he's part of me.

I reach the sofa zone and crawl underneath the big sofa pyramid. I curl up in the dust, making myself as small as I can. I'm such a coward. I hate myself for being so weak, but I can't control the fear monster. His voice keeps bursting into my head. *Of course you're not brave enough to rescue Ada,* he tells me with a laugh.

I wish my parents were here. Dad would give me a hug and tell me everything's OK. Papa would bring me hot chocolate and a snack, then try to come up with a five-stage plan for fixing the situation. But here comes the fear monster to tell me that maybe they only put up with me getting scared because they have to. Maybe, in secret, they discuss me with exasperated sighs. "Shouldn't she have grown out of this by now?" I imagine them saying. What if one day, they shout at me for being so annoying? I wouldn't blame them. *I* want to shout at me.

"She's in here," a voice says.

Emily, Rube and Jack crawl into the dark space to join me. They all sit down and don't say anything, which is the worst thing in the world. I know they're holding back their laughter or, even worse, pitying me for being such a mess.

A big, heaving sob bursts out of me and I clamp both hands over my mouth to stop more from escaping. I've tried so hard to hide how terrified I've been all night. Now I can't keep it inside any longer.

Jack finally speaks. "I admire your dedication, Olive, but your breakdown needs some work if you want to be truly top tier."

"Jack," Emily hisses.

"No, hear me out," he says. "One time, my parents sent me to this activity camp over the summer holidays. Back when everyone still thought I was into stuff like sports and building fires. I didn't know anyone and, on the first night, I was so homesick that I fell to pieces. Like, full on hysterical crying and puking until the camp leaders called my mum to pick me up."

"You were actually sick?" Rube says.

"You've never seen anything like it."

I glance up at Jack. I can't imagine him crying. He's always smiling and laughing. I've always looked up to the popular kids and believed their lives are perfect. Happy, never sad. Hearing how he sometimes cries makes me wonder if he's really so different from me. *You're a million times worse*, the fear monster whispers inside my head.

"Ha, that story's nothing," Emily says. "I had this big race the other month and I got so nervous, I couldn't run. I faked a cramp and then refused to speak the whole way home. Mum was giving me such confused looks in the rear-view mirror."

"Er, where's the drama?" Jack says.

"It was internal drama," Emily says. "Just because I don't show it on the outside, it doesn't mean I'm not a disaster zone inside my own head."

I blink at Emily through stinging, blurry eyes. I can't imagine her being anything less than confident and cool. She's the sort of person who always wins, who never gives up. It's hard to believe she got so nervous that she didn't even try. She gave up, like I did. *Giving up keeps you safe*, the fear monster tells me.

"I cried later, when no one was there," Emily says quietly.

"You should always make sure you cry in front of people," Rube says. "Otherwise, who's going to give you a hug?"

"Says the boy who hid behind a shed when he got upset at school," Emily says, playfully nudging him.

"Yeah, that," Rube says quietly. "Everyone was laughing at me. That's why I hid. Not because of the armadillos."

Jack and Emily go quiet. It's true that lots of people at school laughed at Rube after he started crying. I heard one of the boys calling him a baby. Another kept doing mean impressions of him. *They laugh at you too*, the fear monster says. But for the first time, I start to think the fear monster isn't trying to keep me safe. He's trying to keep me scared.

"My mum says sometimes people laugh because it makes them feel better about themselves. It helps them pretend they don't sometimes feel the same way," Emily says. "I'm sorry I didn't stand up for you."

"I'm sorry too," Jack says. "Why didn't you say something about how you were feeling?"

Rube shrugs. "I felt silly for getting upset about something so small."

"It's not small," Emily says, awkwardly putting her arms around him. She isn't much of a hugger, so this is big for her.

I realize I've stopped crying. I'm still hiccuping on sobs, but everything feels slightly less awful. Their stories have drowned out the fear monster's voice. He's still there, but he's smaller than before.

"What we're saying is, it's not a big deal," Jack says, nudging me. "Getting scared, I mean."

"No one's judging you for being scared," Emily says. "If that's why you ran away."

"We all get scared and cry sometimes," Rube says. He pauses, pulling a face. "Or is the problem that you're an ugly cryer?"

"Rube, seriously?" Emily says. "We're trying to cheer her up."

He shrugs. "I'm an ugly cryer too."

"Everyone is," Jack says. "Except me."

"It's not… It's not that," I say, struggling to get the words out because I'm still doing that horrible gaspy thing. "It's like, I don't just get scared. I get so scared that I … lose it."

They don't say anything, so I presume they're agreeing I really am pathetic and useless. *Told you so*, says the fear monster in my head.

"We all have the things we're good at," Emily says, "and things we're not so great at."

"You're good at ideas and being clever, Olive," Rube says.

"You've talked me out of so many terrible stunts," Jack says. "You think about things. I, um, don't."

"And you're nice to people," Emily says. "You listen and pay attention, instead of only caring about yourself. I like that you don't talk all the time to fill the quiet. I like that you come up with plans to make things happen. I like that I can be myself with you instead of feeling like I'm too serious or too bossy or too much."

I frown, surprised. That's how Emily sees me? As someone who makes her feel comfortable and accepted?

I've spent all this time trying to be interesting enough to keep her as a friend, but that was never what she liked about me. She liked the ... *me* parts.

"You can tell us when you're scared or sad or whatever," Rube says. "You don't need to keep it all inside. I promise no one's going to laugh."

"Not on purpose," Jack says.

Emily kicks his foot. "You're our friend. It's OK to ask us for help sometimes."

I smile. I'm crying again now and my tears feel hot on my cheeks. I still feel a bit silly but, this time, it's because I didn't talk to the others about how I was feeling. I listened to the fear monster instead. But now I can see that no problem ever feels quite so scary once you share it with someone.

It reminds me of how, when I have a bad dream, Dad will turn on all the lights in my room and check under the bed, in every cupboard, and behind the door. Turning on the light and having him there with me is always enough to chase off even the scariest nightmares. The fear monster goes quiet whenever Dad's with me.

Scary things aren't half as scary when you shine a light on them. They're even less scary when you have someone there to hold your hand.

Taking a deep breath, I wipe my eyes. I think maybe it's time to face my fears for real.

"We're going to rescue Ada," I tell the others. "It's time for a new plan."

IT'S DARK DOWN HERE

We peek out from under the sofa pyramid. The coast is clear, but we don't know where Karen is. We need to be ready in case she tries to follow us down into Warehouse Two. We can't have her getting in the way when we rescue Ada.

"First, we need a distraction," I say.

Jack stands up straighter at this. "A distraction, you say? I have the perfect prank in mind."

"Of course you do," Emily says. "What do you need?"

He rubs his hands together. "Someone to run to the canteen and get all the ketchup and mustard."

He explains his idea and we get to work. I remember

watching the *Home Alone* films when I was younger. As an easily scared person, I found all the traps kind of horrifying. Someone could have been seriously injured at any point, if not killed. My parents laughed their heads off, but I couldn't bring myself to find any of it funny. Jack's traps, however, are more amusing.

We unblock some of the paths through the showroom, then Rube strategically places a bunch of sound-activated dancing cacti on various sofas. Jack pinches some Bluetooth speakers from the living-room zone, setting them to max volume. Emily climbs up on to the scaffolding to balance baskets of toys above our heads, then ties strings to them. I scatter balls, building blocks and pineapple ornaments across the floor. We use up all the sellotape we can find.

"One question," Emily says. "How do we get Karen up into the showroom?"

She has a good point. Ada needs us, so we can't wait for Karen to come upstairs by chance. But we can't risk going into the warehouse if Karen's down there. At best, she could interfere with our rescue plans. At worst, she could try to "deal with us" as she keeps threatening.

Rube grins. "I have an idea."

We follow him to one of the desks where people can sit and chat about sofa options with a store worker. On the desk, there's a microphone. It's one of the ones staff members can use to summon their co-workers to help a customer in need.

"What are you going to say?" Jack says. "Go on, make a fart sound."

"You're so immature," Emily says, smirking. "Do it, Rube."

"I have a better idea." Rube clears his throat and cricks his neck. Then he presses the microphone button. "Excuse me, this is Karen and I'd like to speak to a manager."

We all crack up. His impression of Karen is perfect. She's going to be furious.

"I'm up here in sofas right now, and I want everyone to know that I am very, very disappointed with the service I've received today."

"Now make a fart noise," Jack says. He grabs the microphone and blows a long raspberry.

We don't get to come up with anything else as the lift behind us dings. We scramble away from the table and get to our hiding places. I check I have everything I need, then we wait. A few moments later, Karen bursts

through the staff door into the sofa zone looking about as angry as I've ever seen someone look.

Her hair is sticking up in every direction and her make-up is smudged. She's slapping a heavy wrench against her palm.

"Those microphones are staff use only," she bellows.

She's so busy yelling that she doesn't notice the sellotape stretched across the path. She collides with it face first. The tape smushes up her features and sticks to her hair. While she yells and struggles, Jack leaps out from his hiding place.

"Welcome to the show!" he cries, yanking on a string that upends a basket of toy plastic snakes on to her head.

She howls and tries to swat the snakes aside, before realizing they're not real. "You're in so much trouble," she shouts. Producing a box cutter from her pocket, she slashes at the sellotape. She bursts through with a roar.

Emily and I wait until she's almost level with us, then we squeeze two bottles of mustard and ketchup at her feet. The thick liquid splatters all over her shoes and dribbles inside.

"What on Earth do you think you're doing?" she bellows. "This is ridiculous."

She kicks off her shoes, and Emily and I duck aside to avoid being hit with the wrench.

"I'm going to destroy you all," she shouts, moving to come after me and Emily.

Jack steps in front of her and grins. "Shall we dance first?" He presses play on his phone and the Bluetooth speakers we set up start to play "Baby Shark". In my experience, adults think this is the most annoying song in the entire world. The song sets off the cacti. They all light up and start to gyrate while playing back a squeaky version of the song.

"This is noise pollution," Karen cries, covering her ears. "It is completely unacceptable."

Jack waves the phone at her. "Want me to switch it off? You'll have to catch me first."

He runs off towards the dining-room zone and Karen storms after him in her ketchupy socks. It's not long before her screams announce she's stepped on the spiky pineapple ornaments we scattered earlier. That must hurt without her shoes on. Emily high-fives me.

"Let's go get Ada back," she says.

Emily, Rube and I jog back into the living-room zone. We drag a heavy dresser across the path in case Jack can't keep Karen occupied for long. He's under strict instructions to only engage her if he's sure he can get away. If things get too scary, he's going to climb into the rafters where she can't follow.

"He'll be OK, right?" Emily says.

I hesitate. "Yeah, he's going to be fine."

Us, though? I stand at the top of the dark staircase with my hand shielding my nose. It stinks like death.

"Are we really going down there?" Rube whispers.

"We have to," I say.

Before I can change my mind, I lead the way down towards Warehouse Two.

In one hand, I hold my torch. In the other, I have a saucepan. The others are armed too. Emily's taken a tapas serving board from one of the dining tables and is holding it like a bat. Rube is nervously wielding a large wooden fork.

As we descend, I can hear something *drip, drip, drip*. A leaking pipe has made a smooth hollow in

the concrete floor. There's a narrow stream of water running down the stairs. The woodland smell is so strong it makes my eyes water.

"Where are the shadow monsters?" Emily says.

"Waiting," Rube says.

I glance back at them. We all know this is a trap, but it's not like we have any choice. Those *things* have Ada, and I'm not letting them eat my best friend. Because even when I hate her, I still love her. It's very confusing.

We reach a door at the bottom of the stairs. There's nowhere else to go. I push the door open.

We step into a huge warehouse, as big as the one we raced trolleys in earlier. Hundreds of pieces of assembled furniture are crammed in wherever they will fit. Some of the pieces look like they've been down here for years, judging by the dust and the old-fashioned styles. I think maybe they're the old display models from the showroom.

The whole place reminds me of a labyrinth. There are narrow pathways between looming wardrobes. There are dead ends created by piles of sofa cushions and bubble wrap. There are stacked-up chairs that make staircases to nowhere, and upended tables with their legs pointing at the ceiling.

"So this is where they take all the stinky furniture?" Emily whispers.

"Certainly smells that way," Rube says.

"I think they bring it down here and forget about it," I reply. I try to spot the box containing the wardrobe my parents returned, but there are too many to choose from.

"How are we going to find Ada down here?" Rube says.

I gulp heavily. There are so many wardrobes in which Ada could be trapped. The only option is to search them one by one. It feels like such a big task, but then I think about all the times we've played flashlight hide-and-seek, and how I always win because I have a system.

"We need to be methodical," I say. "Open every cupboard and door one at a time."

We set off along a narrow path between furniture. In some places, piles of chairs have been balanced dangerously on top of tables. They wobble when we bump into them.

"Ada?" I call out. "Can you hear us?"

There's no answer.

I climb over an old sofa that's sprouted mushrooms. I edge past a huge wardrobe made of solid wood. I open the doors, but Ada's not inside.

Then I spot something. On the floor, there's a cola bottle. Ada's been dropping them all night, much to my annoyance.

I pick this one up and immediately spot another, and another. "I think Ada's left us a trail," I say. "Like in *Hansel and Gretel*."

"Over there," Emily says, moving towards a path between bookcases. There's another sweet.

"Oh no," Rube says, pointing.

A shadow rises in front of us. It's a goblin, I think. Its head is too big for its body, and it has three chunky fingers on each of its hands. There's a puppet-like way about how it moves. In case you're wondering, yes, I hate puppets. There's something terrifying about the way they look almost human, only *wrong*.

Another puppet shadow appears to our right, and another to the left. All three creatures are here, and we're surrounded.

THE LABYRINTH

We barely have time to scramble on to a coffee table. Biter, Stumpy and Pinky scurry into view with their horrible yellow teeth snapping. They sniff at the air and focus their beady black eyes right on me.

I think of the conversation we had earlier. About how they can hear our fears. But that's not true. It's only my fears they can hear, probably because they're louder than everyone else's. I'm the one that's drawing them to us.

"Listen," I whisper to the others. "You're going to have to go ahead. Follow the cola bottles and find Ada. She's counting on you."

"Wait, what about you?" Rube says.

"I'm going to make sure those creatures don't get in your way. I can buy you some time."

"What?" Emily says. "No. I'm the one with the tapas board, and the good aim. Defending us from danger is my job."

"It's my job to make sure the plan stays on track. This is the only way."

"Look, I don't want to be mean," Emily says, "but we know what happens when you get scared."

"Exactly!" I laugh. "If I'm going to be scared, I may as well use it."

"Olive, I'm not sure," Rube says.

He's not sure I can handle this. But the thing is, telling them all how I feel has made my fears slightly easier to face. The fear monster's voice in my head is quieter than ever.

"You need to find Ada," I tell them. "Trust me, I've got this."

They both nod, unsure. But I know what I'm doing. This plan is going to work. I make sure the creatures are focused on me, then I run. "You want me, so come and get me," I shout.

They chase me, which was the plan. But it's still terrifying.

I clamber over a set of nesting tables and jump down on to a path that leads away from Emily and Rube. There's barely room to squeeze through. Sharp corners and chair legs keep trying to snare my clothes. The creatures scrabble behind me, oozing through tiny gaps.

My heart feels like it's going to explode. I can't outrun them for long, but I just need to get them away from my friends. One of them snaps at the back of my shoe, so I leap on to a sofa and run along the back. I jump on to a kitchen table, sending a box of lampshades tumbling to the ground.

Soon the labyrinth has swallowed me up. I can't see Emily and Rube any more. It's me and a bobbing torch, and the sound of those creatures behind me. I don't look round. I keep running, but then my foot catches on a loose piece of plastic wrap. I trip and go flying.

My knees hit the ground hard. I try to crawl, but I can hear the creatures closing in. There's no point trying to escape. Any second, they're going to grab me.

I think about closing my eyes and clasping my hands over my ears. But it's time to face my fears instead of hiding from them.

I force myself to turn and face the creatures with my torch held high. They pause, then approach me slowly, gnashing their teeth and clacking their long, curved claws on the ground.

This close, they're as ugly as anything I've seen – even the little dog with tufty hair that lives on my street. But I make myself look at them. Really look at them. Their teeth are wonky and yellow, but not exactly sharp. More like a rodent's teeth, designed for gnawing on things like roots. And their long claws are thick not pointy, like they're used for digging.

They stop advancing and stare at me with watery eyes that blink in the torchlight. I think they're used to the dark and the brightness hurts them. All three of them are panting, I realize, not gnashing their teeth at me. Chasing us around all night must have worn them out. They're not very scary now I'm seeing them clearly.

My panic begins to drain away. The fear monster in my head tries to tell me to be scared, but I laugh at him. He's not a big black cloud with a million spidery legs. He's like my dog when he spots a squirrel, barking and growling so everyone thinks he's fearsome. Only he's not.

"You have no power over me," I say, stealing a line from one of Papa's favourite films. The one with the scary goblins, as it happens.

The fear monster backs down and so do the shadow monsters. Their scary goblin shadows shrink to the size of rodents. Without the terrifying shadows, they're kind of cute.

"What do you want?" I ask them.

They don't answer me. At least not in any language I understand. Instead, all three glance up at the furniture that surrounds us. They sniff at the air in a way that looks kind of confused and ... sad?

I think about how they came here from Ipsley Island, accidentally transported to the store with the Flatpack wood. Every now and again, one of them gets sent out to someone's house with an order. I think it might have been Biter who ended up in my attic conversion. And every time, they get returned to the store because the customers don't like the forest-like smell they bring with them or the weird shadows at night.

"Have you been trying to get home?" I say. "Do you climb inside the deliveries leaving the store in the hope one will take you back to Ipsley?"

Stumpy cocks his head at me. He looks almost

hopeful, like my dog does when I open a packet of cheese.

"Is that why you've been chasing us?" I say. "Because you want us to help you?"

I think about how the creatures have been living in this store for years and years, but the people who work here don't know they exist. Then I think about how they didn't reveal themselves to us at first, they just tried to scare us off with their shadows. Then something changed. They started to approach us. We thought they were trying to eat us, but maybe they weren't.

"You can sense all our feelings, can't you? Not only our fear."

I begin to wonder if the creatures heard our friendship in the same way they heard our fear. Maybe they decided they wanted us to be their friends too. The thought makes me feel horribly sad. But it still doesn't explain why they took Ada.

"Where's Ada?" I say, trying to picture her in my head in case that helps them understand.

They all glance behind them, back towards where

we left Rube and Emily. Biter sets off down the path, checking I'm following. I go to stand up, but a sharp pain in my ankle makes me cry out. I must have twisted it when I fell.

Limping, I try to keep up with Biter. He leads me on a short route towards a door out of the warehouse.

"This is where you took Ada?"

They stare at me, which I take as a yes. As I reach for the handle, the door swings open and nearly flattens me against the wall. A unicorn bursts through in a blur of rainbows. Ada, it's Ada! Before I can speak, she grabs me by the arm.

"Karen's coming! Run!" she shouts.

THE SKELETON
IN THE CLOSET

"You're OK," I say, grinning at Ada. "They didn't eat you!"

"No time. Karen's gone full murder mode."

"Karen?" I gasp. "Oh no."

Emily, Rube and Jack appear through the door behind her. Ada drags me back into the labyrinth of furniture. I hobble on my bad ankle, wincing with every step. I don't think I can go far; it hurts too much.

"I couldn't hold her off," Jack says. "I tried, but those meatpops were churning in my belly and one thing led to another."

Karen bursts into the room. "The toilets aren't plumbed in, you disgusting child," she shouts.

Jack shrugs, then rolls over the top of a sofa. I struggle over behind him. By the time Ada's helped me down to the floor, the other three are well ahead of us.

Karen smashes her wrench into every piece of furniture she passes. "Come here," she growls, zeroing in on me and Ada.

"Can you go any quicker?" Ada asks, frowning as Emily, Rube and Jack disappear into the labyrinth, leaving us behind.

"You can go ahead if you want," I say. The pain is making my voice shake. "You don't have to stay with me."

"Yeah, I do," Ada says, rolling her eyes. "Especially seeing as you came down here to rescue me. I didn't need rescuing, by the way."

My heart sinks a little bit. She isn't even slightly pleased to see me. "How did you get away?" I ask.

She steps over a broken footstool. "The creatures teleported me here, then led me to the delivery bay. It took a lot out of them, though."

"Maybe that's why they had to use you as bait. They wanted the rest of us to follow you down here."

"Except, they're not the monsters you all think they are."

"I know that," I say snippily. "We were communicating. But then you burst in and they vanished."

"Communicating?"

"I think they want us to help them get back to Ipsley Island."

"So that's why they took me to the delivery bay," Ada says. "That must have been how they arrived here in the first place and they're hoping we know a way to send them back."

We reach a dead end. There's a tall pile of chairs, but I don't think I can climb it. Karen's wrench slams into a bookcase, making us jump. Her face appears in the space between two wardrobes, all of her teeth bared.

"Got you now," she says, waggling the wrench at us.

I scream and we quickly change direction. Ada pulls me through a narrow gap Karen will struggle to fit down. We reach a huge wardrobe that smells like rot.

"Get inside."

"What? No!"

"Come on. Before she sees us." Ada opens one of the wardrobe's doors and pushes me inside. It stinks, and it's darker than dark without our torches. We can't risk Karen spotting the light through a gap in the wood.

Ada quickly pulls the door closed. We stay as still as mice. Karen is close by. I can hear her footsteps. There's another bang as she smashes her wrench into a piece of furniture. A door opens, then closes.

"Where are you?" Karen yells.

We listen as she continues to search for us, her footsteps gradually getting quieter, then louder again as she comes back. I cross my fingers that she won't try to search inside this wardrobe. It's set back from the others. Maybe she'll miss it.

But Karen's footsteps come closer still. Ada shifts position and her unicorn horn nearly takes my eye out. I shuffle over and bump into the person on my other side. Except…

"Ada?" I whisper. "There's someone in here with us."

"What are you talking about?"

"There's a person sitting right next to me," I say through gritted teeth.

She switches on her torch to the red-light setting and slowly lifts it. It illuminates a skeleton. An actual skeleton. The only thing holding him together is his Flatpack uniform. The badge on his chest reads:

"It's … it's Marcus Knight," I say.

"I can see that," Ada says, leaning across me to get a better look. She doesn't seem in any way bothered that there is a dead person in this wardrobe with us. If anything, she sounds curious.

"Maybe the creatures teleported him here and forgot about him," I whisper, but it doesn't feel right. There has to be another explanation.

Right then, there's a huge crash. The whole wardrobe shakes. The wooden door cracks, then splits. Karen yanks both doors open, grinning like this is the best day of her life.

She looks terrible. Her hair is sticking up in a hundred different directions and her make-up has smeared into demonic clown territory. "Got you!" she says, slapping her wrench against her palm.

I panic and grab the first thing to hand – Marcus's skull. "Catch," I say, throwing it at her.

She bats the skull into the air with a shriek and drops the wrench. Ada and I try to slip past while she's distracted. We don't get far. Karen grabs our clothes and lifts us both off the ground. She's much stronger than I expected.

"Oh no you don't," she says, throwing us back into the wardrobe.

My head clunks against the wood and I cry out with pain. Karen smirks and reaches down for the wrench.

This is when the truth hits me. She genuinely wants to hurt us. Not just scare us a bit. We're in real danger.

Whenever something bad's happened in my life, grown-ups have been the ones who've fixed it. My parents, my family, my teachers at school. Even strangers. One time I knocked myself out falling off my bike, and the man who mows the grass called an ambulance and held my hand until Dad arrived. Another time I got lost at a music festival, and the woman making flower headbands looked after me until my parents found me.

I took it all for granted, like that's the way the world works. An adult will automatically help a kid who's in trouble, right? But seeing Karen's evil smile and the wrench in her hand, I'm realizing this isn't true. There are some awful people in this world and Karen's one of them. The fear monster in my head doesn't need to say anything. This is real.

Without taking her eyes off us, Karen picks up Marcus's skull with her free hand. "Oh, Marcus, you're disgusting," she says, pulling a face.

"It's ... it's sad, isn't it?" I say, thinking I can appeal to her humanity. Maybe if she understands the true horror of death, she'll think twice about hurting us. "You were friends, and now he's gone forever."

"Friends?" She raises an eyebrow. "Business partners, more like."

"Business partners?" Ada says. "Marcus Knight was part of your plot to steal from Flatpack?"

She laughs. "It was his plot, if I'm completely honest. But I don't have to split the profits any more, do I?" She throws the skull over her shoulder. I flinch at how callous she is.

"She's not even surprised," I whisper to Ada.

"So?" Ada replies.

"What's that?" Karen says. "Speak up."

"I said, 'you're not even surprised Marcus is dead'," I say. "You're not going to ask how his skeleton ended up in this wardrobe? It doesn't bother you at all?"

She purses her lips at us, then sighs heavily. "No, not really."

My brain whirs as it tries to make all the pieces of this mystery fit together. The shadow monsters aren't actually monsters. They're definitely not murderers.

So who killed Marcus? The most likely suspect is the one who stood to gain the most from his death.

"Did you ... did you kill him?" I say.

Ada looks at me sharply. "What?"

"Like she said, she doesn't have to split the profits any more," I whisper.

Karen laughs. "Kill him? Of course I didn't kill him!" she says. "No, I just locked the wardrobe door and left him here."

Hearing her admit it feels like the downward rush of a roller coaster. My last little piece of hope that she will let us go home falls away. She's the real Flatpack monster. She murdered Marcus so she could take over his criminal enterprise. Now she's going to have to kill us too, if she wants to get away with it. And there's no one coming to save us.

"I knew no one would find him down here. They won't find you either," she says gleefully, reaching for the wardrobe doors.

"Olive?" Ada says shakily. "Now would be a good time to come up with a plan."

I have nothing. I try to come up with something to

keep Karen talking while I think. "We're children," I blurt out. "They won't give up looking for us like they did him."

She pauses with her hand on the wardrobe doors. "There's no CCTV footage and no one knows you're here, do they?"

Neither Ada nor I say anything. Karen's right. We were so careful about not letting anyone else know we were coming here. My plan made sure of it.

Karen tries to close the wardrobe doors. I put my foot in the gap. "Are you honestly planning to murder two eleven-year-olds? Think about it for a moment."

She does seem to think about it, but then she shrugs. "It's not really murder, though, is it? If I lock you in a wardrobe and you can't get out."

"That's still murder," Ada says.

"Definitely murder," I add.

"Is it, though? Is it really?"

"Yes," we both say.

"Oh. So be it."

We both scream as Karen slams the doors closed, then turns the key in the lock. We try to push the doors open with our feet, but the wardrobe's too well made. It's not lost on me that this has to be the one piece of Flatpack furniture that isn't constructed from flimsy plywood.

Karen chuckles to herself. "They'll never find you in there."

I hear sounds like furniture being dragged across the floor. Something heavy bumps against the wardrobe. Karen's barricading the doors so we can't get out. We kick and scream, but it's no use. She's shut us in here and now we're going to end up skeletons like Marcus Knight.

NOT THE BLANKET BOX

I'm breathing so fast I'm sure I'm going to pass out.
My thoughts are spinning out of control. I can't stop
thinking about who will actually miss me. Have I made
enough of an impact on the world for anyone to care?
The fear monster in my head doesn't think so.

"Are you OK?" Ada says, switching on her torch.
It lights up the inside of the wardrobe – and Marcus's
headless skeleton, lying slumped in the corner. I think
the darkness was preferable.

"No," I manage to choke out. "I'm not OK."

I half-expect Ada to mock me for being such a baby.

To my surprise, she squeezes my hand. "You'll come up with a plan. You always do."

I shake my head. "Not this time."

"But—"

"Can you please leave me alone, Ada? Please."

She goes quiet. We sit there, shoulder to shoulder, in awkward silence. It's hard to pretend someone doesn't exist when they're locked in the same tiny space as you, but I do my best.

"Look, Olive, I—"

"I don't want to hear it!"

"I'm trying to say I'm sorry. I said some mean things to you and they weren't true. I only said them because I was angry."

I almost laugh out loud. Ada's sorry? I don't think I've ever heard her use that word before.

"I do sometimes act like it's the Ada show," she admits. "I don't mean to do it. I have all these things to say, and they all just come out."

I go to say something in reply, but I have nothing. Of all the surprising things that have happened tonight, Ada apologizing has to be the most unexpected. I feel like a punctured balloon. All the anger rushes out of me and I'm left all limp.

"I took it for granted you'd always be my friend," she continues. "But about a year ago, you started getting distant. It was like you decided you think I'm as annoying as everyone else does."

"It's not that I think you're annoying," I say quietly.

"You don't have to lie to me. A murderous Karen has locked us in a wardrobe. It feels like a good time for the truth."

She's right. If I've learnt anything from telling Jack, Emily and Rube about my fears, it's that scary feelings stop being so scary when you share them. So I take a deep breath and tell Ada the truth. "I got it into my head you only liked me because you had to. Because our parents are friends," I say.

"Really? But that's so silly!"

She doesn't need to tell me it's silly. I know it is. I still feel like it's true, though. Why would someone like her like me?

"I worry about things," I say. "I get things in my

head and then they're all I can think about. That's why I got distant."

"Oh. Right. You know, you could have talked to me about this."

I wipe away a tear. "I thought you'd laugh at me."

She seems to consider this. "I'm not laughing now."

"No, but this isn't exactly a laughing situation." I rap my knuckles against the wood surrounding us.

She chuckles at this then trails off. "Can we fix this, Olive? You and me, I mean. I'd really like to be friends again."

It's funny. For months, I've felt like there was nothing in the world that could make me want to be friends with Ada again. But now I can't see any reason why we wouldn't be friends.

I try to answer, but my breath is shaky and I can't get the words out.

"I can be a better friend," Ada says. "Less weird."

"No!" I say. "You don't need to change anything."

"Neither do you," she says, squeezing my hand. "Let's be weird together."

And like that, I have my best friend back. She hugs

me and I don't even care that her furry onesie tickles my nose. She doesn't let me go for a long time.

"We do need to come up with a plan, though," she eventually says.

Suddenly, there's a horrible scream from somewhere outside the wardrobe. "Get off me, get off me," Karen screeches. "No, not in the blanket box."

A lid slams. A muffled voice shouts. Feet kick out against wood.

Ada and I wait, holding each other tightly. Then there are more voices and the sound of furniture being dragged again. Finally, a key turns and the doors open. I throw myself out of the wardrobe, gasping in deep breaths.

"You're all here!" Ada says.

At first I think she means Emily, Jack and Rube. The three of them are standing outside the wardrobe, looking worried. But they're not alone. Biter, Stumpy and Pinky are here too. Squinting up at me with watery little eyes.

"Um, so the monsters shut Karen in a box," Jack says. "It was epic."

"The twins are in boxes, too," Rube adds.

A large wooden chest bumps and shudders as Karen screams to be let out. Emily kicks it. "Be quiet," she says. "We're trying to have an emotional reunion."

She heaves me off the ground and hugs me so tightly I can't breathe.

"We thought you were both behind us," Rube says. "I'm sorry we left you."

Ada pats him on the shoulder. "You came back, that's what matters."

"Of course we did," Jack says. "That's what friends do."

"Ahh, group hug?" Rube says.

There's not much room, but we manage to all squeeze in close, with our heads together and our arms around the people next to us. I'm sandwiched between Emily and Ada. It's funny. I always thought I had to choose between them: the old friend or the new friend. But now I realize I can have both.

"I'm glad we came here," I say.

"Seriously?" Jack says.

"I mean, there have been some parts I wouldn't want to experience again. Ever. But … you know."

"Ahh, we love you too, Olive," Rube says.

"You know what I love?" Emily says. "My bed."

Ada laughs. "I never thought I'd be the one saying this, but let's go home."

Three little creatures squeeze into the middle of our circle and look up at us hopefully. Biter snuffles at my shoes.

"We need to help them get home first," I say. "Back to Ipsley Island."

ORDER PENDING

In the delivery bay, there's a small office full of loose paperwork and dirty mugs. There's a computer and a printer. I sit on the swivel chair and move the mouse. The computer lights up.

"What are you doing?" Jack asks.

"I'm going to divert an order to Ipsley Island," I say.

The program Flatpack uses to track packages and generate postage labels is still open on the computer. It doesn't take me long to work out how to use it. I change the delivery address on a wardrobe order. Hopefully no one will notice until it's too late.

A printer whirs to life. Emily takes the label as it emerges. "You're posting them back home," she says.

"That's such a clever plan."

"One of my strengths," I say. "We need to find order number 2311-6543-004R in the packages awaiting collection. It's going out tomorrow morning, so we need to make sure the creatures are inside."

I glance at the doorway. Biter, Stumpy and Pinky are shyly watching us. I worry they won't understand, but they follow us into the delivery bay. Their claws clack on the floor, but it's no longer a scary sound.

There are several metal racks lined up by the back doors, containing dozens of packages. It takes us ages to find the right one. Emily sticks the label over the original and then opens one end of the box. The creatures immediately squelch inside, squeezing into a far smaller space than should be possible.

"I wish I'd had the chance to find out more about them," Rube says sadly. "They really are fascinating creatures. Their existence changes everything we know about life on this planet."

"We can't tell anyone about them," Ada says quietly, like it's a thought that's just come to her.

I look across at her sharply. "What happened to

proving the existence of a new species?"

Ada hands Emily a roll of tape so she can close the box. It looks like she's trying to hold back tears. "They deserve to live in peace. Knowing they're safe is enough for me."

"Um, seriously?" Jack says.

"Yes, seriously. Besides, there are other undiscovered creatures out there," she says. "And we're all such a good team—"

"No," I say. "Absolutely not." I can guess what she's about to suggest, and I'm not even going there. I march out of the delivery bay and go in search of the stairs that will lead us back up to the showroom.

Jack and Emily catch up with me. "Come on, Olive. It will be fun," Jack says. "Think of all the footage we'll get."

I shake my head. "Nope. It's not happening."

"You were the one who said you're glad we came here tonight," Jack says.

"You've got to admit that tonight was kind of fun," Emily says. "In parts."

"Fun?" I say. "You think this was fun?"

Ada and Rube join us, and Ada throws an arm around Emily's shoulder. "Don't worry, we'll win her over."

We emerge from the staircase into living rooms. Immediately, I hear voices in the houseplant zone. Torches cut through the plastic jungle. We all freeze as a short-haired woman emerges through the leaves. She's dressed in cargo shorts and a tucked-in shirt, and has a keychain lanyard jangling round her neck.

Jack shrieks. "Oh no, it's a new Karen!"

The woman shoots him a cold look and raises a walkie-talkie to her mouth. "I've found the kids in the living-room zone. Over."

"Auntie Sarah?" I say in disbelief.

The woman isn't a Flatpack worker. It's one of my dads' friends. What on Earth is she doing here? It's not only her. Other people quickly come running from all directions. There are dozens of people in the showroom, all of them with walkie-talkies and torches.

"Mum?" Jack says, squeezing past me. "Mum!"

Everyone's parents are here, along with pretty much everyone who's ever been to one of my dads' BBQs. They must have called literally everyone they know to come and look for us. And they all turned up!

I peer through the torch beams until I see them. My

parents, running from the kitchen zone with looks of terrified hope on both of their faces. Then they spot me.

"Olive, you're OK!" Dad almost tackles me and drags me into a suffocating hug. I burst into tears. We're safe. We're going home.

It's a few minutes before Dad releases me. That's when I notice Papa's eyes are damp with not only relief, but also fury. And I remember the part where we lied to all our parents so we could come here tonight.

My heart sinks with shame. We're in so much trouble.

IT ALL TURNS OUT OK IN THE END

My parents realized something was wrong at about nine p.m. They'd tried to message me goodnight and, when I didn't answer, they phoned Emily's mum. That was when they discovered I wasn't sleeping over at her house, and all our lies unravelled. I guess my plan wasn't such a good one, after all.

Papa called Ada's parents, and they called Rube's parents, and Emily's mum realized Jack had to be involved too. Then everyone's parents called everyone they know, asking if anyone knew where we were. In a funny twist of fate, it was me – the most unmemorable person in the world – that someone remembered seeing.

They'd spotted me in the Flatpack car park, picking up some dropped litter and putting it in the bin.

After that, Dad tried calling the Flatpack helpline, and then he called the police, and then he assembled all his friends to form a search party. The rest is history, as is my belief that no one would even notice if I went missing. Clearly there are a lot of people out there who care about what happens to me, which makes me feel kind of warm inside.

It doesn't make me feel warm inside when I think about how much I worried my parents. Obviously, they forgave me. They couldn't stay cross when they found out about Karen and the twins. They definitely couldn't stay cross when we told them about Marcus's skeleton in the wardrobe.

But a week later, I still feel guilty. So guilty that I've grounded myself. Dad and Papa say I'm allowed to go out and see my friends, but instead I've spent most of my time cocooned in my bedroom. I feel safe here.

I'm lying on my bed when my phone rings. It's Ada. "Did you see the news?" she says before I can even say hello.

"What news?"

She sighs dramatically. "The Flatpack factory on Ipsley Island has been abandoned. The report said it was because dangerous levels of some toxic chemical have been found in the soil. But I did some digging online and there are rumours the workers all walked out two days ago. They claimed the factory was haunted."

I smile. The wardrobe delivery containing the creatures arrived on Ipsley four days ago. I guess our new creature friends immediately got to work scaring off all the Flatpack workers. Hopefully no one will return.

"Now the people are gone, Biter, Stumpy and Pinky should be safe," Ada says. "A happy ending for all."

"Not Karen," I say. "Dad told me she's been charged with murder, attempted murder, tampering with evidence and theft. The twins will probably go to prison for helping her."

Ada sniffs. "I still say we should have left them in their blanket boxes for a few days. It would have served them right."

I can't argue with that. Since that night at Flatpack,

all my nightmares have been about Karen trying to murder me. I told my friends and they all said they've been having bad dreams too, so it's not only me. That makes me feel slightly better.

"Moving on," Ada says, "I've been thinking about what creature we should go in search of next. I heard a rumour about possessed badgers, so that's a definite possibility…"

I smile to myself as Ada gets carried away telling me all her ideas. It's like old times, but better. Nothing's changed and everything's changed.

ACKNOWLEDGEMENTS

My first thank you goes to the team at Scholastic for giving me the opportunity to horrify a whole new age category of readers. As always, it's been a joy working with my brilliant editor Lauren Fortune. Thank you also to Sarah Dutton, Wendy Shakespeare, Nicki Marshall, Christine Modafferi, Jamie Gregory and everyone else who has worked on this book. I am beyond delighted to see my words brought to life by Robin Boyden's amazing illustrations and the prettiest book cover I've ever seen. Also, the hugest of thanks to my agent, Chloe Seager, who is literally the best.

I am endlessly grateful to the librarians, bloggers,

booksellers, educators and reviewers who have supported my previous books. Another big thank you goes to all the readers who've bought my books and helped me turn what started out as a hobby into a career. And to my writer friends: thanks for your advice and cheerleading, and for putting up with all my angst.

Finally, a big shout-out to Phill, Eliza and Max. None of this would be half as fun if you weren't here to share it with me. I'm so happy that I've finally written a book you can all read without me worrying that I'll have to deal with the nightmares.